THE SEARCH FOR LANA

N. A. Le Brun

ISBN: 9781549517938

This book is dedicated to the following people:

KS – you have always supported and advised me with my endeavours.
JDV – you never stop reminding me I can do more than I think.
Mum – because of you the vraic is in my veins.
CC – you have changed my view of so many things over the recent years, especially of myself and what I'm capable of.

PROLOGUE

Hi, my name's Lana, at the moment as I write this I'm not that much older than you I guess, I just turned sixteen last month, but I'm not sure when you'll be reading this. I guess I could very well have left the physical life and entered the next; you may very well be older than I am now. But as the next in my family line you need to know as much as I can tell you about where you came from. Mum and Dad adopted me when I was six weeks old; my biological mum wasn't ready to have kids - she was only fifteen when she had me - just a little bit younger than I am now. I guess you can say that I've had a pretty average life, my adoptive parents and their kids (I have two older brothers, James and John, identical twins and an older sister, Sam) have always treated me like one of their genetic family, and through that I have always felt relatively normal. I say relatively because, well you'll see why. Even before I knew I was adopted, I knew that I was different - the twins and Sam always did averagely at school, and although all three of them did extra-curricular activities, none of them exceedingly outshone the others. Me on the other hand, well let's just say I've always been a little above standard. I'll never forget my old school teacher, Mrs Warburton's face when she asked me to read a passage of my reading book to the class - it was Dickens's "Tale of Two Cities" - I was six. Well there you have it, my reading skills were advanced, and so was just about every other skill I had. My parents and teachers called me 'gifted' I called myself a 'freak' and so did half of my classmates when they realised that I was too able. Which is why, at the age of fourteen, when the story really begins to develop, that I had few friends, and even at the all girls school for bright students I attended, I was considered an outsider.

CHAPTER ONE

The New Teacher

I was in year ten, and taking GCSE drama. For arguments sake we'll say that it was a Monday morning, although now I can't be sure, however I do know it was November and our first day back after the half term holiday. A new teacher arrived that day, her name was Mrs Rachel Higginbottom, and she was aged about fifty with grey hair, glasses, and about five foot six tall. We were performing duologues that day, and I was half way through my performance with a girl called Joanna, when she walked in. Just as we finished, Miss Carols called the class over and introduced us to Mrs Higginbottom. The new teacher's eyes were a deep blue, and they swept around the class, smiling as they went. However, as she reached mine, her eyes lingered, making a connection that I still find hard to describe, even though I know more now than before, but I'm getting ahead of myself. The feeling, as best as I can explain it, was as if she was staring into my soul, and at the same time triggering some long lost memory, so distant that I couldn't quite reach it. As the connection was severed, and she surveyed the rest of the class, I couldn't shake off the feeling. The only thing I remember her saying when she was introduced was "Call me Mrs H." I managed to suppress the semi-queasiness from when our eyes had locked, however, until the end of class when the bell rang for morning break. I put my books into my bag and headed towards the connecting door to the canteen.

"Lana, could you come here a second?" It was Mrs H.

"Yes Miss." I reluctantly answered, after all she was a new teacher, what could I have done to upset her; I'd only known her five minutes. Then again, with some teachers that was all they needed for me to have upset them, they tended to get sick of me knowing the answers to all of their questions pretty rapidly.

"Don't worry, you've done nothing to upset me," she assured me in a calm, mother-like tone.

"You...you..." I stumbled, it wasn't a good idea to let her think, let alone know that I was a freak.

"Yes, I can read your thoughts, yet I see you haven't developed that area of your mind yet, unusual in a girl your age. Never mind, I can help you with that if you decide you want me to."

"A girl my age...it's as though you think it's normal for people to read other people's minds!" Was this woman for real - read someone else's thoughts? Me?

"I know it's a shock, but you'll see with time that you are different to everyone else around you, and with good reason, telepathic skills included." She spoke gently and calmly, as if she had all the time in the world.

"It'll take time, but you will see that I am right." She had to be joking, either that or I was dreaming, 'cos there's no way that she could know everything, right? Wrong! And apart from that I already knew that I was different.

"I'm not joking, and you are not dreaming.

I can assure you of that. Now, let me see…" she paused for a moment, and again those blue eyes pierced me in an indescribable manner. "…You have always been slightly advanced for your years," Slightly! Talk about understatement!

" …And you have been bullied or outcast for most of your life by those you consider your peers. You long to be 'normal', and not a freak. Am I right?" She couldn't have got closer if she would have jumped into my skin and walked around as me for a day! Even though the situation scared me, for some peculiar reason, I trusted her, she seemed concerned rather than patronising, it was just that I couldn't get over how my peculiar inclinations appeared to her as nothing other than normal. This was weird.

"I…I…" the bell rang again, "I'd better go." I mumbled as I hurried to the door, slinging my forgotten bag over my shoulder as I went.

"Come and see me at lunch, Lana, I think we should talk." She called after me as I made my way down the corridor, through the locker room and to my next class.

*

It was with some reluctance that I returned to the drama studio that lunchtime, surveying the familiar black walls, the door in the corner that adjoined the canteen, the green filing cabinet in the left hand corner by the door to the locker room corridor, the lighting desk on the right, and the black shelves sagging under the weight of books, the only place at school, where the girls saw me as normal - maybe it was because in drama nobody acted like a regular fourteen year old. My reluctance wasn't due to the fact Mrs H was strict or beastly like Ms. Lawson, the cyborg maths teacher from hell who hated everyone and everything, especially me - she wasn't, neither was she as scary as Mr. Portland the English teacher who had supposedly worked for some secret government agency - it was just that, well, how many people are you likely to meet in one lifetime that can describe you and your life so far in the space of five minutes of knowing you? My guess up until that day would have been none. I knocked on the drama office door timidly, the office itself, no bigger than a walk-in closet, was and still is the least scary place I have ever been. Only accessible through the drama studio, it had two desks squeezed inside it, and there was definitely no room to swing a cat - not a hobby I'd suggest, cats aren't toys, as my brother James found out, Suzie, Sam's black cat ran away and never came back after James tried that one. Anyhow, I knocked and waited, no answer. I knocked harder, nothing. I opened the door, an empty room, if I was to leave, I could just tell her I forgot, or the truth - she wasn't there when I showed up so I left...damn!

"Lana, so glad you decided to come." I swung round, and there she was, her hair piled on top of her head in a bun that resembled a pale pineapple.

"Yeah...I guess" What was I doing? I mean after all it could have been a daydream, right? The earlier conversation I mean.

"Well perhaps we should sit in the studio, it's a bit cramped in the office." No I hadn't been dreaming. "Take a seat here, and I'll be with you in a minute."

I sat in the corner nearest the canteen door, half hoping to escape, and wishing I was with Catharine (one of the few friends I did have at school), eating the veggie lasagne or whatever was on the menu that day that could be eaten with an extra large portion of chips, followed by chocolate cake. However, I resigned myself to the fact that I wasn't, and sat apprehensively. Seconds later Mrs H walked in, carrying a small wooden box that looked as if it was about a hundred years old, the wood was darkened with age, and the thick iron hinges were worn and rusty. She sat down beside me, laid the box in front of me, and told me to open it. I looked at her questioningly and thought, 'She's barmy, nice enough, but positively barmy.' Even with this thought running continuously through my mind, I couldn't resist the strange temptation I felt as I picked up the box and ran my finger along it's dust-encrusted lid. As I did so, I felt a slight indentation. Using the sleeve of my school jumper I wiped away the grime and uncovered the apparent engraving. It was written in French, a language I had learnt from primary school, and had again excelled in; "Les secrets des Magiques. La boite de la famille Cornique" (The secrets of the Magiques. The Cornique Family Box, I could have translated the word 'magiques' but it felt wrong to do so, more instinctive than anything else). I gently lifted the iron latch, and opened it under Mrs H's watchful eye. Inside, it was lined with a material that was an exquisite shade of purple, unlike any I'd ever seen, not aged like the exterior, but new in appearance, yet I had the feeling that it was just as old. Another thing occurred to me, it was bigger on the inside than the outside, no, that couldn't be right - yet it definitely had to be. "Things aren't always as they seem" Mrs H had picked up on what I was thinking. On the top of the box, there was a leather bound A4 size book, with the words 'La Famille Cornique' embossed in fading gold leaf on the front cover. I removed it from the box and gently opened it, inside on the yellowing pages were photographs of people smiling back at me. I could only presume they were the family whom the box and album belonged to. They dated back to the eighteen hundreds, and as I flicked through the pages, the peculiar distant memory feeling hit me again. I reached more modern photos; a younger Mrs H stared up at me, followed by her children on the following pages. A sandy haired young man called Timothy, according to the name underneath the picture, an equally sandy haired girl called Kara, and two dark haired girls called Monique and Tillie, who were obviously identical twins. The lost memory feeling grew stronger as I looked into Tillie's piercingly sad eyes that stood out from an otherwise smiling face, the only difference that was contained within the pictures of the twins. My stomach churned as I looked down into the deeply concerned eyes of an otherwise stunningly beautiful young woman, who, at the time of the photo couldn't have been much older than me. In fact I wasn't sure that she was, everyone in the album seemed to be my age or thereabouts. I turned the page again, half expecting it to be blank; I dropped the album in shock as my own face peered back at me. The bell rang; I had to go to Science. We arranged to meet after school, with the promise that my presence in the album would be explained. Had I found my grandmother? If so was it pure chance, or was there something going on that I couldn't quite grasp?

As it happened, Mrs H cancelled the afternoon meeting by way of a letter she'd left for me on top of her desk. I arrived at the drama office to find the letter and album on her desk:

Dear Lana,

Sorry to tell you like this, but I forgot that I have a meeting to go to. Please take the album and look at it again. Don't concentrate on the pictures too much, look at the empty pages at the back, and remember, things are not always what they seem.
See you before school tomorrow,

Rachel Higginbottom.

Where had I heard that before! I was exasperated, I wanted answers to my questions, and instead I had an old photo album, full of people I didn't know - great! However, I picked up the letter and album, and slipped them into my rucksack, and went outside to wait for Dad on the front steps. I decided not to tell anyone at home about the album, there was no need to alarm them, and I mean, after all, I might be jumping to conclusions, this might be coincidence, and the girl in the photo may

just look like me and share my first name.
Irrational thought process I know, but come
on - I was confused. Dad showed up in the
family Carolla, and as I jumped in alongside
him, I forgot all about the letter and the
album.

*

It wasn't until a dinner of homemade
sausage casserole and generously sized
dumplings (how I love Mum's cooking!),
that I went up to my room and opened my
schoolbag ready to do some homework. I
walked over to the window, turned the
heater up a notch, and then flicked on my
stereo. I grabbed a CD off the shelf, and
soon my room was filled with the music of
Boyzone (my fav boy band at the time), I
reached into my bag, and grabbed
everything out of it and piled my work onto
the desk. The album and letter slipped from
my grasp and landed on the floor, the album
had landed with the back cover open, and a
blank page staring at me. Ignoring the letter,
I turned back to the more recent photos of
Mrs H and her kids, and of course, the girl
who could have been my twin. It was

irrational to think this anything other than coincidence, after all I had never even met Mrs H until today, so it couldn't be me in the photo! I quickly closed it again, pushing it to the side of my desk and pulling out the maths homework that was due in the next day. Higher-level maths GCSE was perhaps the wrong maths for me to be taking, the homework, which allowed a calculator because of its difficulty level, was easy to do and within five minutes I had finished it without the need of the calculator. I hated it; I wanted to be like the other girls, not do it, get into school, and rush to finish it, gaining a lower grade than potential allowed. But it was like I was differently programmed, and I was bound not to have that as a possibility, it would be another one hundred percent, 'Excellent work Lana! Why can't you girls be more like Miss Le Monnier here?' Another reason for them to hate me at school, teacher's pet again! All apart from Catharine, she always stood by me, still does, even though we haven't seen each other much recently, but I'm getting off the point. With my maths done, I concentrated on my English assignment, turned on my laptop, and finished off the essay that wasn't due in for another week. My homework, which should have taken most of the night (according to those who had set it, and probably would for the rest of the girls in my various classes) but was finished in half an hour. That night I really longed for more, I was trying to ignore the album which sat on the corner of my desk, and I found that I couldn't any longer.

Perhaps a drink, that'd help, it'd calm me down, and give me an excuse to get out of my room for five minutes or so whilst I went downstairs to the kitchen, found a glass, poured myself some coke and came back upstairs. However, I still ended up back in my room, with the glass sitting half drained on the coaster on my desk. It was no good, I couldn't avoid it forever, picking up the album, and I walked over to the bed, and collapsed on my duvet. Placing the album next to me, I cautiously opened the front cover, each photo appeared to have been taken in the same place, a place which seemed familiar, but one I was sure I had never been, yet even my photo, or the photo of my double, was in front of the same backdrop, a wall with a fireplace that seemed as if it were in a family home. I felt like I was prying into someone else's life, it wasn't right, and yet, I couldn't bring myself to put the book back in my bag. The photos contained a familiarity, one that in the context of me and Mrs H was obvious, I knew me, and I'd met her, the rest, I couldn't explain, especially the instinctive feeling that her daughter, Tillie was someone I wanted to hug and never let go. I flicked through the empty pages, which filled the rest of the volume, lingering on the second to last, examining each and every square inch, as if it hid some detail, some long forgotten memory which my mind had locked away, and needed to be discovered now. The longer I stared at it, the more I felt it, and without my knowledge, the further my eyes drooped. It wasn't until Mum woke me up the next day, shouting that I was going to be late for my seven-thirty play rehearsal that I realised I had fallen asleep.

*

I got to school, just in time for rehearsal, and to my great surprise ran straight into Mrs Higginbottom. That was the last thing I felt I needed, if I did not hurry I was going to be late, and Miss Carols would kill me, there was only a couple of weeks until the school production, this year it was a musical version of 'Twelfth Night', and as Viola, I had more than enough to do, including sing a song about the dual roles my character was playing. Whilst it was another thing I excelled at, I hated singing in public (still do), but Miss Carols and the music teacher Mr Delaney had insisted that I take the part, solo and all, as it was in a range that varied too much for the others in the cast to accomplish. My argument had originally been, you wrote it, you can change it, but Mr Delaney said he had written it with me in mind, and I couldn't turn him down, he was one of the few people at school who believed me when I said I hated being top of the class and over-achieving, and had taken pity on me when my classmates made fun of me - he told me they were jealous and that I needed to concentrate on the friends I had (you know what? He was right, teachers and adults sometimes are). Mrs H smiled when she saw me,

"Don't worry, you're not going to be late, I'm heading to the hall myself, I'm assisting Miss Carols, she's worried about

the chorus work, and I offered to help."
Typical, the one place I thought she wouldn't
be, and she was! Rehearsal sped by, and I
promised Mr Delaney I would practice my
solo during music class at three-thirty.
Another thing about being gifted, I was
doing all the GCSEs offered, not just the ones
I wanted to, and yet I still seemed to have
more time than anyone else, maybe because I
finished the work set in class and the
majority of the homework in class time.

I managed to escape without Mrs H
catching up with me, which for all of ten
minutes seemed like a blessing. I got to form
and sat down, waiting for Mr Atkins to come
and take the register. My form teacher was
as dull as dishwater; he spoke in a monotone
voice that sent my form to sleep, and left me
in a state of semi-consciousness. His tweed
suits had stereotypical leather patches on the
elbow, and he took the whole of form time to
read the register.

"Lana?"

"Here Mr Atkins."

"We established that five minutes
ago, are you alright?" Mr Atkins looked
generally concerned for the first time in his
life. " I was calling out Cassie's name."

"I'm fine Sir, mustn't have got enough sleep last night." Great, another thing for Cassie, the most popular girl in school to make fun of, she would probably start telling everyone that I wanted to be her, which was as far from the truth as it got. But I could have sworn somebody had just called my name.

"Lana, keep quiet and listen. It's me, Mrs Higginbottom." Ok! I was freaking out; I knew perfectly well that she wasn't in the room. I definitely hadn't gotten enough sleep.

"Why do you assume that you're freaking out? I did not get a chance to ask you to hang around after drama, during lunch so we can continue our discussion." Something was definitely not right; I obviously had Mrs H on the brain that had to be it. I managed to shrug off the weird experience I had just had, and made my way to English with the rest of the class.

CHAPTER TWO

History Lesson

It wasn't until after break, which I spent with Catharine in the canteen, going over our play lines that I found myself stuck in the position of remembering the earlier freak out I had had in form. I had decided not even to tell Catharine, after all, my best friend may have accepted my normal level of freakiness ('normal', yeah!), but this was just too weird. As I entered the drama studio, I noticed it was already half full with about two thirds of my class, and although the majority of them despised me, I felt peculiarly safe knowing that because they were there meant that there was no way Mrs H would be able to grab hold of me without raising suspicion, which was something I instinctively knew she would not want to do.

Class went without a hitch, it was theory mixed with practical, learning the ins and outs of the lighting system. It was a basic system, which the school could not afford to replace until the next academic year, non-computerised and totally manual, I had been using it since I was in year seven, and the lesson thoroughly bored me. The others however, were having difficulty in comprehending the way in which you faded the lights without having to bring down all the switches, and as Catharine pointed out to me, a goldfish could have realised there was a fade button, and as you probably know, they have an extremely short memory span. It wasn't until the end when Catharine and I were voluntarily shutting down the light deck and taking the lights off their stands that I began to feel vulnerable again. We managed to put them all safely next to the filing cabinet and were just about to go and grab lunch when Mrs H came out of the office. "Lana, aren't you forgetting that we'd arranged to go over your extra assignment?" She asked looking at Catharine.

"I'll catch you later." Catharine said to me picking up her book bag and heading through the door.

"Catharine wait!" It was too late, the door had swung behind her and I was trapped. "Mrs Higginbottom, we never arranged…"

"Do you not remember me asking you earlier to stay behind?"

"But…but I thought…" So she had infiltrated my mind; that felt horrible, in fact it felt down right rude.

"I'm sorry, I did not mean to upset you, but I couldn't have asked you in front of the class, I did not want to create even more stormy waters between you and them." Wow! She was thinking about how it would affect me if the popular girls found out! Yet I was still kinda annoyed with her, I mean wouldn't you be?

"I'm sorry Mrs Higginbottom, whilst I'm grateful for that, I still don't see why you couldn't have just found me at break, I mean it's weird enough that you seem to think that I'm perfectly normal, but I mean to talk to me when I was in another part of the building was bizarre. It just isn't normal!" I hadn't meant to blurt out my feelings like that. Why had I? It wasn't like me to do that, unless I was talking to Catharine, and the past couple of days I had been careful about what I was telling her, and this 'extra assignment' meant I would have to lie to my best friend, and that was something I was dreading, as I knew it was wrong.

"Normal, that's something you strive to be isn't Lana. You cannot accept these wonderful gifts you have. I thought you would have wanted to know why you are the way you are. Maybe I was wrong." Her words cut me like a knife; it wasn't that I did not want to know. I had wanted to find out who I was since I first found out that I was adopted. It was just too much too soon. Those blue eyes looked at me with such disappointment that I felt guilty and angry with myself. I did not know why, but for the first time in my life I truly felt, not empathised with, the pain of another. I had to say something, but what?

"Mrs Higginbottom, please don't think that I don't appreciate what you're doing, I just had a bit of a shock. I mean, I'm fourteen and have had to learn to put up with being outcast, not just because I'm adopted and look nothing like my adoptive family with their red hair and green eyes, and their stocky build, but because of my 'gifts' as you call them. And suddenly you come along with apparently all the answers I've been searching for since I discovered I was adopted and it wasn't some genetic throwback that made me so different from my family, and I got completely freaked. I'm sorry, I did not mean to upset you." I rambled out my feelings for the second time, I hated myself for hurting her.

"It's ok Lana, it's ok." She put her arm round my shoulder as I started to weep with the power of the combined pain that I felt. "I shouldn't have said what I said, it was wrong of me. I didn't think before I spoke. That was my fault and I'm sorry for that." Hang on she was apologising to me for being upset, that wasn't right.

"But I upset you, and people do say things when they are upset! It was my fault, I was being an irrational teenager."

"You were reacting like any normal teenager would. There goes that word again - normal. The only thing you truly share with your peers is the hormones that rage through your body. But you already knew that." She seemed to have rid herself of the hurt, and appeared to be tired. Not sleepy-tired, more tired within her soul. She had had to deal with rebelliousness from her children, and whilst I was not rebelling in the traditional sense of the word, I could tell this was familiar territory for her.

"I've got to go and get the books for my next class. My music lesson's only half an hour and Dad doesn't finish work until six-thirty tonight, so I won't be leaving until about quarter to seven to get to my dance class. Why don't we talk after Mr Delaney's class?" I couldn't believe I had said that, let alone how calmly the words had come out of my mouth, and the fact that I really, truly felt that it was the right thing to do, not only for her, but for me as well. My first moment of teenage rationality.

*

My afternoon English class was a bit of a blur, mainly because my mind was racing with the thought of what had happened at lunchtime. I had made my first adult decision, and not only was that not meant to happen for another couple of years, but a proper adult had accepted it. I had started off the lunch hour as a teenager controlled by hormones, but finished it a young adult controlled by her mind and heart. My music lesson at three-thirty was monotonously slow, as I had finished the term's work in the first half term and Mr Delaney had me practising my solo for the whole half an hour, regardless of the fact I knew it by heart, and as he admitted at the end of the session, I could have sung it backwards, with the tune in perfect reverse order. I was apprehensively desperate to get to the drama studio, and ran from the music block, through the modern languages department, past the humanities department and down the main staircase to the drama studio in thirty seconds flat. A distance, which usually would have taken about fifteen minutes to walk. I arrived in the drama studio to discover Mrs H sitting in the middle of the green carpet, going through the contents of the wooden chest with a sad smile on her face.

"Lana, come sit with me. I'm so sorry about earlier, I hope you don't think that I was trying to pressurise you into meeting with me." She was truly frightened that my suggestion to meet was made out of guilt.

"No, that's not why I said we should meet. I acted like a spoilt brat earlier, I really do want to learn what you have to teach me about who I am."

"Well that's nice to hear." She still looked unsure, as if she felt I did not want to be there and was merely humouring her. "Perhaps we should continue to go through the box. But first, have you got the album with you? I'd like to fill you in on a few things." I pulled the album out of my rucksack and sat next to her.

"This album contains photographs of my family from as far back as possible. I know that that may shock you in regards to the latest one it contains, but you need to know why your picture is contained within the pages." It was true, it had to be, I had found my grandmother; my heart surged with the sudden rush of adrenaline that raced through my veins. "Two hundred years ago, my family settled in Jersey. My ancestors had previously travelled continuously, trying to find a place they could call home. It wasn't easy for them to leave their original homeland, but they had to because of fear of persecution. Their motherland was under the influence of an oppressor known only as The Sergeant. He had overthrown the royal family, and they and their supporters found it increasingly difficult to remain. It was through the help of a few elderly scientists that they managed to escape and begin the search for a new home." She paused for a minute, stood up, went into the drama office and put the kettle on. It was obviously hard to discuss the family history, and so far what she had told me had been genuine, of that I was sure, yet I did not remember France being under a dictatorship, it certainly hadn't been in any of the text books I had read, and I had read more than my classmates put together. She came back in with two cups of tea, and resumed her position on the carpet.

"It was an eternal struggle to find a new home, each new place was treacherous in its own way. Some places were uninhabitable, some were under the influence of The Sergeant, others disapproved of my family's gifts, and there were other lands where the inhabitants were not as advanced as we were and would have caused us to regress into a fairly primitive state or otherwise they would have gone into a state of culture shock, the differences were far too great. Jersey was perfect, it was small, but not to small, had vast areas of countryside for us to settle in, the people were content living simple lives, but were also part of the industrial revolution, they were aiming to better themselves and keep up with the technological revolutions which would make life easier whilst embracing the nature that existed alongside them. Even though we had to keep our more challenging gifts a secret from our new neighbours, their spiritual beliefs were different from ours and things could quite easily have gotten awkward. We found that we could live without too much scrutiny, and were generally accepted." Wow! So far an amazing story, yet I was no closer to the answer I wanted, no, the answer I needed. Was I staring at my grandmother in complete rapture, or had I been jumping to conclusions? It was my turn to get up and straighten my legs, as Mrs Higginbottom sipped her tea; I walked around the studio, digesting what had been said waiting for her to begin again.

  "Maybe I'm giving you too much information at once. Perhaps…"

  "No! Don't stop. I need to know and I still have a couple of hours. Please Mrs Higginbottom, go on." I couldn't believe that she was about to stop I needed the information.

"As long as you're sure then. The lives of the ancestors were undisturbed and the surrounding households soon started going to them for minor medical aid. Most in the country could not afford the doctor and my family were happy to help with anything that they knew could be cured by simple herbal remedies. Whilst they held the power to do more they were not willing to show themselves as full-blown healers as that would have given their whereabouts to The Sergeant, which was not an option, as he would have dragged them back, and they would not have survived his torture. Life was more relaxed than it had been for years yet they still had to keep their guard up, one slip and they would be discovered. The Sergeant was and still is an unknown entity whose lifespan is greater than that of any human race. It may be that he still lives, we cannot be certain that he doesn't. All we know for sure is that he still holds a great influence over our homeland, dead or alive and because of that we cannot return." She stopped and sighed heavily, her mug, half full lay forgotten in her hand. Mrs Higginbottom obviously had not told anyone this tale for a very long time and it was taking its toll on the sprightly middle-aged woman. I allowed a pause in the conversation so that Mrs H could relax a bit before plucking up the courage to ask the question that had been on my mind for the past hour.

"Mrs H, I need to ask, when was France under such a dictatorship and how can it still be? My history books have never mentioned anything about it, and I've read every single history book in the town library. I know without doubt that you are telling me the truth as I see it in your eyes and feel it within me yet I am having trouble placing what you have told me in context as it doesn't tally with my knowledge of European history."

"My ancestors were not from France, Lana. Although that is the language they spoke." Mrs Higginbottom gazed again into my eyes and I could tell that she was silently questioning as to how much further she should go. "However, now is not the time to tell you exactly where we came from. You may feel ready for it but I see that I was right; your mind needs time to process the information I have given you. We will stop for today." Ordinarily I would have argued against this as I often did when authority figures told me I did not need to know any more. I did not because I knew that neither of us held the physical or emotional strength to continue. Mrs H because recounting the family history was obviously painful, and me because my mind was beginning to overload on what I had been told and also because I couldn't bear to let her go through any more emotional distress at that moment. Instead I chose a different route and followed the train of thought that had been running simultaneously to the previous question.

"Mrs Higginbottom…"

"Call me Rachel, Lana. It's not the school day any more and we share more than just a teacher-student relationship. You and I both know that." She smiled a gentle, grandmotherly smile.

"Rachel how did you know…how do you know so much about me? How are you so sure that I am the person you should be telling all this to and that you shouldn't just be teaching me GCSE Drama like you are the rest of the class?"

"Call it intuition, Lana. I know that

that is the easiest way for you to understand why. It is a context you will have a ready grasp of. My family would call it 'la persipacité sixiéme'. In short we instinctively know when there is another 'Magique' within the same room as us. Also you are of the right age for...well...no now is not the right time. Speaking of time I have to get home. Take the album back home with you and study it some more. Wait here a minute." She picked up the chest and mugs and headed to the office coming back out holding an envelope. "Give this to your parents. They will know what it means. I must ask you not to read its contents as your parents will tell you what they decide you need to know from it at the moment. It may be frustrating for you but the answers you seek will come when you are ready to deal with them."

*

I got home that night after the shortest ballet class on record. Mrs Morris, our class pianist, went into labour half way through the first set piece and class came to a complete stop. Even if the broken tape

player had been working none of us had the
capacity to continue, as we were more
concerned about Mrs Morris. Dad picked
me up and we stopped at the Chinese to pick
up the takeaway Mum had ordered. She
never cooked when I had dance classes or
the twins had rugby practice or Sam's riding
lessons happened after school and usually
these after school activities fell on the same
night. We got home, washed up and sat
down to dinner. It turned into the normal
free-for-all that happened every time the
twins sat down to a meal. I had no chance to
quietly hand Mum and Dad the letter from
Rachel whilst James and John fought over
the last spare rib and Sam whinged at Mum
over the cost of her horse's food bill and how
it was becoming greater than she could
afford on her part-time job as well as all the
other equestrian bills she was paying. I
quietly finished eating and grabbed my
school bag before heading up to my room. I
was tired beyond belief, my mind consumed
by the heaviness of my earlier conversation
with Rachel. She had had a hard time telling
me as much as she had and yet I couldn't
help being slightly angry with her for not
telling me more. There was also the fact that

there was something between her and my parents. My life seemed to be disintegrating instead of becoming more fulfilled as I had expected it would. I removed the envelope from my school bag and ran my fingers over its edges, aching for a clue to its contents. I couldn't open it because I'd been asked not to and couldn't break the trust that had been placed in me but the temptation to gain the knowledge it held was driving me to distraction. I opened the door and poked my head through the crack and onto the landing, the envelope still in my hand. My parents and siblings were still downstairs. Sam was continuing her discussion of equestrian expenses and it sounded as if Dad had eaten the last rib in an effort to stop the argument between the twins but it had backfired and they had now joined forces and were yelling at him instead. Now was my chance. I snuck down the landing to Mum and Dad's room and placed the letter on Mum's pillow. When I got back to my own room I collapsed on the bed and passed out with mental and physical exhaustion, it had been an extremely long and hard day.

*

A couple of days later I went downstairs after my usual Saturday morning lie-in to discover that my siblings, instead of watching Saturday morning TV had disappeared out of the house extremely early. Mum and Dad were sitting in the kitchen huddled over the table talking in hushed voices with a third person. And if I wasn't imagining it, my persipacité sixiéme was telling me that the person was a Magique. It wasn't Rachel of that I was sure and it made me uneasy. I knew that she (I could tell she was female by her voice which joined in the conversation at odd points), was related to Rachel and therefore possibly a member of my biological family if Rachel was indeed the matriarch of my true family.

"She's in the lounge." It was the woman, either she had raised her voice or I had been listening closely enough to pick up on it, I wasn't sure. However, I do know that we felt each other's presence as clear as if we were standing next to each other and it made me slightly uncomfortable.

"Lana?"

"Yes Dad?"

"Can you come here for a minute

please? There's someone we want you to meet." There was something severely wrong with this. My parents hadn't mentioned Rachel's letter since I had placed it on their bed. It was as if it had never existed and now there they were, in the kitchen with a member of her family, waiting for me.

"Coming Dad." I sounded far happier than I felt. My heart was beating so fast and hard that it could have broken each and every one of my ribs. I walked through the doorway and kept myself from looking at the woman who sat in Mum's chair.

"Lana this is…"

"Monique Higginbottom, Rachel's daughter." I turned to face her. "But why is it you that's here? You're not meant to be here! It should be your mother to come and discuss the situation!"

"Lana, don't be rude." Mum tried to stop me from behaving so confrontationally. Looking at her I could see lines appearing on an otherwise youthful face and it suddenly dawned on me that the reason the letter hadn't been discussed was because my parents had spent every waking moment trying to work out what to tell me.

"It's ok Gwen, honestly. Lana has

every right to be angry and hurt and upset."
Monique was defending me and yet I
wanted her to disappear and for her mother
to be sitting in her place. "Lana why don't
you sit down. You're right that it should be
Maman, not me sitting here. Unfortunately
she has some family business to take care of
that couldn't wait."

"From what I gather this *is* family
business! Although I'm not sure who my
family is at this moment! Mum, I know that
you and Dad love me as your own but I'm
pretty sure that both you and the
Higginbottoms are keeping something from
me and I don't think that's fair! Like for
instance the fact you seem perfectly cosy
sitting here with Monique and don't seem
totally phased by what is turning into the
biggest thing I've ever had to face! In fact
you seem more worried about how it is
going to reflect on you two when the whole
thing is out in the open!" I was absolutely
livid and for the first time in my life angry
with those I love most. My parents
exchanged worried looks and yet Monique
remained as calm and cool as a cucumber. I
was more infuriated than ever.

"Unless I get some answers and unless you

stop acting as if my behaviour's totally normal, Monique, I'm going to go and ring Catharine and see if I can move in with her because I know that she wouldn't keep this sort of secret from me!" I had temporarily forgotten the explaining I would have to do when Catharine found out about all of this.

"Lana, look, we never wanted to keep anything from you. We thought we were doing what was best for you and the Higginbottoms agreed." Dad spoke up for the first time since I had entered the room. "Why don't we all have a cup of tea and something to eat and then we can continue in a more civilised manner and maybe Rachel will have arrived by the time we finish." That was news; Rachel *was* coming she was just running late.

"That would be lovely Jack. Milk, no sugar for me." If she did not wipe that smile off her face I was going to do it for her!

"Lana, what about you? Orange juice and a bacon sandwich?"

"As long as it's the veggie stuff I guess I could eat something." I wasn't even hungry but I needed to take my mind off Monique's annoyingly calm composure.

"I don't understand you darling. You

hardly ever eat proper meat nowadays and when you do it's usually the smallest amount possible." Mum looked concerned more than anything else and I think she was trying to change the subject, which in my opinion was the best thing she could have done.

"Mum, I eat enough meat and fish to keep you and the doctor off my back and to gain what I need from a varied diet but I just cannot agree with the way in which everyone insists that I eat something that I do not enjoy."

"But you used to love a proper fry-up and you always used to beg me for a bacon or sausage sandwich when you were younger."

"That was before I started to take care of my health. I need to stay away from too much cholesterol and want to eat healthy. I only allow myself one fattening meal at school a week and one at home. I enjoy my salads and the other healthy meals I have and my only weakness is two small bars of chocolate a day. If I want to continue dancing and acting I need to keep my body and mind fighting fit."

"She has a point Gwen. If she feels

that she wants to eat healthily we can't stop her and after all she might just pull the twins into eating their veg by setting a good example." Dad came back with my OJ and my veggie BLT.

"I doubt it Dad! They won't touch anything that isn't covered in sugar or deep-fried and you know it!" I had started to calm down and was steering clear of any conversation linked to Monique as her mere presence was causing the hairs on the back of my neck to prickle in anger. There was something distinctly wrong with the woman sat at my table and it was more than I could quite grasp at that moment. As I relaxed a bit, I felt a further presence on its way up the garden path. I quietly excused myself and headed to the front door. I opened it and there stood Rachel looking as if she was about to ring the doorbell.

"Oh so you decided to show up then!"

"I'm sorry I'm late Lana but I had some things to deal with. I trust Monique explained my absence." Rachel seemed generally concerned and my disgruntled feelings towards her simply vanished although I still felt annoyed with her daughter. "Shall we go and find your parents then?" I showed her in and we headed for the kitchen, the only trouble is, Monique and my parents had vanished without trace.

CHAPTER THREE

La Grotte

"Mum? Dad? Monique? Where are you?" I started to tear round the house searching for them but I couldn't see them anywhere. What was going on? This couldn't be good and I wasn't the only one who had gone pale at the unexplained disappearance of the three adults who had been sitting in the kitchen. Rachel had collapsed into one of the armchairs by the electronic fire in the living room. She suddenly looked old, older than her fifty-odd years and it was weird to see the spirited middle-aged woman looking so aged.

"Lana, where are your siblings?"

"James and John are probably at a friend's house and Sam's probably down at the stables with her horse."

"Ok, they'll be alright where they are. I'll give them a ring later and see if they can stay out tonight. We'll explain everything to them once I've figured out what's going on. For now we need to get you out of here and somewhere safe." She did not explain why and I did not ask. I knew that Rachel would explain in time and I was too shocked at what had happened to question her. My parents had vanished along with Rachel's daughter and I was having trouble trying to understand things in my own head. The only thing I knew was that I was positive that Monique had something to do with it and I couldn't shake the thought out of my head.

*

The drive to Rachel's house was the most sombre occasion of my short life. I couldn't bring myself to talk and Rachel was muttering something under her breath in French. I had shouted at my parents! I had told them that I wasn't happy with the secrets and now I did not know if I was ever going to see them again! Why had I been so rude and uncooperative? My heart was

beating ten to the dozen and I felt wretched.
My life had definitely taken a turn for the
worse. Pulling up to the house I wondered
how many times I had been in the car with
Dad when he had driven up this way in
order to pick Sam up from the stables. I had
never before noticed the quiet little
farmhouse that stood slightly off the road. I
had been too busy singing along to the radio
or discussing the latest book I had read
instead of taking in the countryside around
me. Now I regretted not paying more
attention to the surroundings, maybe my
persipacité sixiéme would have picked up
that my family lived within a stone's throw.

Before I could take my seatbelt off Rachel
ordered me to stay put. She ran into the
house and came back carrying a huge
wooden chest with what seemed like great
ease. It was at least fifty times bigger than
the small one she had shown me in school.
She put it in the boot and climbed back into
the driver's seat.

"If he found you there we're not safe here
either. The others will know what is wrong
and in case I'll send them a message. We
won't be able to come out of hiding for quite

some time."

"Hiding, now wait a minute! I cannot simply leave my brothers and sister on their own with strange things going on and then there's school. There is no way!"

"Lana we have no choice. You're brothers and sister will be fine, I've arranged for them to stay with your Aunt Sophie for now. I know you don't want to let Mr Delaney and Miss Carols down but we have to hurry. Trust me on this." Rachel was not making much sense and yet she was. I knew she was right we had to go. We drove to an obsolete area in the middle of one of the Northern parishes. We abandoned the car behind a bush and carrying the chest between us we walked for what seemed like an eternity. Eventually reaching what could only be described as an overgrown and forgotten dolmen. We set the box down and Rachel whispered into the wind:

"Ouvrez pour moi, ta maîtress." The smallest boulder shook violently and suddenly moved about ten feet to the left and a stairway appeared at the top of a very long tunnel. Between us we carried the chest down the stairway stopping only for Rachel to close the doorway. The stairs seemed to wind on for miles and the further we went the colder the stone floor and walls became. There was a small amount of moss growing in the gaps between the granite. The further into the depths we plunged the more light we seemed to encounter. It was created by hundreds of burning torches that increased in number with each few hundred yards. By the time we reached the bottom we were in a circular room surrounded by eight or nine hearths burning brightly with orange flames. It was warmer here than above the ground and appeared to have been turned into a lounge area with tunnels shooting off here and there leading to other rooms. The room was big enough to fit my entire school year inside and contained several large chairs and sofas. It was beautiful.

"Welcome to La Grotte, Lana. This place has been in my family's possession since they emigrated here in 1865, about thirty years before I was born. My father found it by accident and developed the network of caverns that create the homestead."

"It's very cosy and homely down here. Hang on did you say your father? That'd mean that…" I must have heard her wrong, because that would have made her at least one hundred years old and there was no way that that was humanly possible.

"Yes I did say my father. Lana do you remember me telling you that things are not always as they seem? Well that's by and by, there's something else which we need to discuss. But first how about we unpack and have some lunch." I looked at the clock over the fourth mantelpiece and then decided to check my watch instead. The clock had thirty-six hours around it instead of twelve and what could only be described as the second hand was moving three times as fast as it should have been. It did not faze me as much as it would have done a couple of weeks ago but I still couldn't read it. My watch told me it was nearing two o'clock and perhaps Rachel was right we needed to eat something.

*

Lunch went past quickly and so did the unpacking. To my great surprise Rachel pulled my small suitcase out of the chest with a few of my clothes packed into it and the album, plus my rag doll 'Delphinine', the only item I owned that my biological mother had given to me. And a couple of my schoolbooks, I wasn't going to have to neglect my studies after all. Just miss out on the play! It wasn't as if I had wanted to sing in front of everyone, just that I hate to let people down. My pain at disappointing Mr Delaney and Miss Carols was soon stopped by the realisation that my parents needed me more than I had ever needed them. That and the things that kept coming out of the chest, there were hundreds of things that I had never seen before, an instrument with four or five sundials connected to each other, wooden bowls with symbols carved into them that appeared to represent the four elements and all sorts of wonderful contraptions that were too strange to describe in words. Then there were about four-dozen books with nothing written on the black binding but they seemed to bulge with information. There was also food, enough supplies to fill a supermarket. There were bags and bottles containing herbs and salt and water and charcoal and all sorts of ingredient-like items. The final things to come out of the chest were twenty brooms with twig ends and eight highly polished sticks. The chest had held more than it

should have been able to, even with its large
size. I instinctively knew that it was as it
was meant to be and that I should stop
questioning how and start asking why things
were happening.

*

We sat down by the fire nearest to the
stairwell drinking huge cups of mint tea.
Every now and then the wood in the fire
would spark and send out a flurry of
crimson flames. The coal in the next fire was
of a particularly gaseous batch as it kept
sending blue-green sparks onto the rug
covering the stone floor. It was comfortable
in the large armchair with its patchwork
covered cushions and had my mind not been
racing through everything that had
happened in the past week it would have
been enough to send me into a deep sleep. I
couldn't have cared less that I was
underground and that this would become
my home for the foreseeable future and
whilst I had not seen the rest of La Grotte, I
felt safe. That however was part of the
problem I was sure that while I was safely
stowed within the belly of Jersey my parents

were somewhere else and possibly in danger.

"Rachel, I… there was something wrong with Monique this morning. She seemed…" I couldn't even be sure what was wrong but I felt it deep within me that she wasn't acting normally and it wasn't just my annoyance at discovering her within my house.

"Go on Lana." She turned to face me for the first time since we had sat down.

"It's just that, well, she was too calm." It sounded daft, even to me but I was sure she should have been more exasperated at my tantrum than she was.

"I see what you mean. She lacked emotion didn't she?" Rachel placed her mug on the small table that lay in between the two chairs.

"Well frankly yes." What was going on? How did Rachel know?

"I feared that this might happen. It's one of the reasons I was late this morning, I needed to check a few things out."

"Like what?" I was longing to know what had been so important and Rachel seemed to resign herself into telling me in a rather straightforward fashion.

"Lana, when I asked Monique to go for me this morning and make my apologies I never realised that I was endangering you and your family. It wasn't until I placed her laundry on her bed before heading to yours this morning that I had discovered what I done. I found in her room something I thought she would never have owned. It was a small mirror with the markings of The Sergeant around its frame. My daughter is in league with him, for how long she has been his spy I do not know but she has compromised our very existence, yours included."

"But why mine? I mean what threat do I hold to him? I never even knew about any of this before this week!" I couldn't believe what I was hearing. Why would Rachel's daughter betray her own family and why betray me?

"Lana, I cannot believe I am having to tell you like this, but you were right, I am your grandmother. I wasn't sure how to handle the situation at first. Your mother was not quite sixteen and I was angry with her. It was hard to accept that one of my children would be silly enough to fall in love and have a child at such a young age."

"Wait, you mean that Monique…"

"No. Monique is not your mother. She is your aunt. Your mother is…"

"Her twin, Tillie."

"Yes. Tillie is your mum. She begged me to let her keep you, but I couldn't agree with her. I loved you dearly, but I knew that for both the sake of the family and your survival we would have to give you up."

"But why? Why was it so important to remove me from my family and place me with another? I don't understand how anyone could do that to a child they loved!" I couldn't believe what I was hearing. Kind and gentle Rachel, my own grandmother, had torn me from the arms of my mother.

"Lana, I must ask you to stop interrupting. I know you have many questions but hopefully they will all be answered before I finish." I nodded and signalled that I would remain quiet. "I'm sure that you remember me telling you how the ancestors came to live in Jersey," I nodded to show that I did. "Well there were four generations travelling together. The older ones died within four decades of arriving. The need for them to protect the

family had become less great and their
spirits gave up the struggle to stay alive.
The last one of these was my grandfather. I
was just a little girl when he passed away,
but I remember the conversations between
him and my father. They talked daily of the
homeland and how my grandfather wished
he could return. The trouble is once royalty
has been dethroned it cannot be sure of its
own safety." Hang on, I was royalty? "They
both knew this and it saddened my
grandfather greatly. Anyway, in one of the
last conversations the two of them had
discussed a prophecy that had been made by
one of the old ones before she had died. It
stated that one of the daughters of the last
daughter of the first son of the last king
would give life to a female babe who would
have the ability to conquer The Sergeant and
his hold over Laterrétoile, our home planet.
Yes I did say planet." She had seen me raise
my eyebrows in disbelief. "The thing is, my
father was the first son of the last king and I
was his last daughter, his youngest child.
The prophecy also foretold that the child
who would be our potential saviour would
be born to a daughter not yet out of her
second decade. In other words, Kara was

too old to have the child, as she was twenty-one when you were born and I knew that Monique despised the very idea of having children. You were to be the daughter of Tillie, my youngest (admittedly only by five minutes but she is my youngest daughter). If I knew about your potential power then it was possible that so would The Sergeant, I couldn't keep you with us as I wanted to. We had to give you to another family, just until you were old enough for the truth to start coming out. However, I did not want to have to burden you with the whole truth at once but it seems that La Mére Eternelle has decided that I must." This was way to surreal! Up until today I had been freakish Lana, the girl who always did well at everything, had been sure that I had found my family and had been on the brink of discovering that I had potentially more talents than I thought but I was *not* ready to discover that I was the prophesised saviour of a planet I had never heard of! My life was already weird enough!

*

If I was to believe everything I had

just heard my life as an outsider was sealed
and I was way past the point of no return.
The thing is, ordinarily I would have
laughed off what I just heard and woken up
from a bizarre dream and life would have
been as normal as it ever had been.
However that was not to be. I knew that
Rachel would not lie to me and that was
what was making the situation harder to
accept. If she knew all this then so did my
adoptive parents and that was where a lot of
the anger lay. As much as I love them with
all my heart, at that moment in time I was
not only worried about their safety, but I was
also furious with them for not telling me the
truth about my genetic family. Even though
now I look back and see that they were
doing what they and Rachel thought best, I
could not help the need to lash out that I felt
stirring within. The trouble is I did lash out -
at Rachel.

"Why the hell did not you tell me all
this years ago?! You and my supposed
parents have been keeping this from me for
years and then you go and tell me that not
only am I your granddaughter but I'm the
prophesised saviour of a race of people I
know nothing about! What do you expect of

me? That I'll know exactly the right way to do everything and that I'll be happy to do everything that's asked of me just because your great-great-great-grandmother or whoever she was told your grandfather that I'd defeat The Sergeant? Hello I think that maybe I should've been asked if I wanted any of this thrown at me and if I want to have anything to do with this at all!" As you can see my newfound teenage rationality escaped me during this brief explosion and my hormones had taken full control over my conscience. And as I would have expected her to, Rachel took it all in her stride.

"I understand your anger at what I have told you, Lana. But you will need to face your destiny. Without you there may not be many lives left at the end of The Sergeant's reign, including your parents. I had no intention of dropping it all on you in one go, I would have preferred to build you up to it, but unfortunately I had no choice. Carry on shouting at me if it will make you feel better but eventually you'll get tired and that won't change how you feel, in fact it will only make you feel worse. I've got the time to sit and listen if you want to continue." She had silenced my temper in one swoop.

She was right shouting wasn't going to get me anywhere. As for accepting my destiny I wasn't sure if I could do that at that point. It was going to take time for me to adjust. "Why don't I show you your room? You can unpack and then we can prepare dinner." She lead me off down one of the passages, carrying my suitcase in one of her hands and one of the polished sticks in the other. Every time we reached a torch burning in its holder she muttered under her breath and it lit. I marvelled at this sight, but it was nothing to compare with the complete awe I felt when walking into my room behind her. The room I was in, despite being a cave was an exact replica of my room at home. The only differences were the torches burning on the wall and the fact my bedspread had been changed. In front of me lay all my possessions. Yet they couldn't have been - I'd left them all at my parents' house. I ran my fingers over the desk surface, it had to be mine, it had the same scratchy lettering from when it had been in the tree house and John had tried to carve our names in it when we were little. He had done it on the first day I had climbed up the ladder into the house. My parents had freaked out it was my second birthday. The memory brought tears to my eyes and I had to tear myself away from the desk. It was painful to think of happier times when right now I did not know where my parents were. I collapsed onto my bed and picked up Delphinine out of the suitcase and burst into loud sobs. I couldn't believe that in a few short hours my life had completely turned upside down.

*

It was whilst we were preparing dinner that Timothy and Kara turned up, dragging two heavy trunks down the stairs. Both bore huge smiles exactly like they had been wearing when the photos in the album were taken. The only difference apart from the fact that they had aged was that Kara now sported the short spiky hair and Timothy's sandy locks were tied back in a plait that reached the backs of his knees. They looked like they had decided to swap the roles of brother and sister. I was in awe of these two figures. My aunt and uncle as I now knew them to be were the epitome of cool! Kara had earrings hanging from every available space in her ears, and showing from underneath the top that barely covered her midriff were two tattoos and a bellybutton piercing. Timothy had tattoos on both of his arms, there was a wolf baying at the moon, a nymph sitting at a waterfall and numerous others. I could tell that the tattoos joined into one big picture on his back, but couldn't see them as his sleeveless t-shirt covered them. Rachel had a different view of things.

"Kara, you look so boyish with that haircut! Can't you grow it out? And as for you Timothy, do I spy a new tattoo? And can't you cut your hair to the length Kara's got hers?" It was obviously a new attack in a war waged against her children's appearances.

"Maman, chill! We're comfortable like this. Apart from that, do you really expect me to be the girly-girl that Tillie and Monique have always been? I thought you liked people to be individual. What's for tea? I'm starving!" Kara was used to the onslaught from her mum and obviously had prepared her answer. She smiled at me, turned around, lifted her top and showed off a tattoo of a beach sunset. Turning back to face me, Kara held her finger to her lips and winked. I could tell that I was going to like her.

"You must be Lana." Timothy beamed at me, showing a perfect set of white pearly teeth.

"Yeah, that's me."

"Well I'm Tim. Glad to meet you." He stretched out his hand and took mine, shaking it vigorously. His hand was rough in places, what felt like the scars of eczema positioned at odd junctures on his skin. I felt an instant love towards him and Kara.

"Maman you're not cooking meat are you? You know I'm vegetarian!" Kara sounded exasperated. And I found that I had something in common with my aunt.

"No I'm not. I'm doing veggie alternatives. Lana doesn't like meat either. Like aunt like niece I guess." Rachel gave me and Kara a stony look that did not reach her smiling eyes.

'So...so...you've...'

"Yes she's told me! All about the prophecy and everything!" I smiled as Tim's face turned into a picture of amazement at the fact that I had picked up on his thoughts. Admittedly it shocked me slightly at first. It was the first time that my mind had picked up the thoughts of another without them entering my mind first. My skills were developing and it hadn't taken that long. I wasn't sure if I could control them but it was nice to know that I was not the outsider with my biological family too.

"Maman, I thought that, well you know. Only the matriarch could pick up on the thoughts of others without meaning to. You know, part of the whole Magique thing." Ok so I wasn't normal - great a freak yet again.

"Kara do you not remember that when you started reading minds the same thing happened to you to? Honestly, kids!" Phew! I was normal.

"Oh yeah... kinda. And what's all this about being a kid, I turned thirty-five last month!"

"You'll always be my daughter and therefore my child." Rachel smiled. It was nice to be part of a normal family scene where I was not constantly aware of the fact that whilst I was loved I was totally and utterly different. That night I sat down to a meal with people who knew what it was like to be ostracised by society for their gifts and who seemed more interested in the habits of an everyday family than why I had a higher intelligence and physical ability. The fact my adoptive mother and father had been abducted by one of my biological aunts was pushed to the back of my mind, I was content with for once being normal.

CHAPTER FOUR

Lessons

After a long and satisfying night's sleep I woke to wonder why I was asleep in my bed yet in a cave at the same time. For a moment I thought I was still dreaming, that is until I rolled out of bed and landed on the stone floor with a thud. At the same time Kara came in carrying two large steaming mugs of peppermint tea and a tray of cinnamon buns. As much as I love my herbal tea, I could have done with a strong black coffee and a couple of ibuprofen tablets as my backside was killing me. But that aside my spirits were soon revived as I ate and drank. I was so intrigued by Kara that whilst I ate I kept asking her questions.

"How come Rachel disapproves of your haircut and tattoos so much? I think they're cool!"

"Why thank you sweetie. I think Maman's more upset about the tattoos than the haircut, not to mention the piercings. We were always told as kids not to draw attention to ourselves and Maman still doesn't accept that tattoos and body piercing are part of the norm nowadays. I have to admit, I was pretty much like you when I was younger, and so was Tillie, neither of us wanted the gifts we were born with, we just wanted to fit in. But unlike you we had the rebellious streak from the moment adolescence hit as we had the biological link to fight with." At these last words I felt a sudden sadness sweep over me, during my years spent without my mother or any contact with my birth family I had found it impossible to rebel. "I'm sorry, I wasn't thinking."

"No, no it's alright. What about the hair, is that rebellion too?"

"No it's not. It's just part of the tomboy in me. That and the fact my boyfriend likes it this way." I nearly spat my mouthful of tea across the room. But thought better of questioning my aunt. She had delivered it so matter-of-factly that I knew not to respond. I guess I just hadn't figured on her having a relationship. I changed the subject:

"Any news on my mum and dad?"

"No. Although Maman thinks they're somewhere between here and Laterrétoile and I'm sure she's right. She nearly always is. There's no way Monique would have been able to meet with other agents of The Sergeant otherwise. Don't worry though; we'll work out some way of getting them back in one piece. Anyway, Maman said that as soon as you've finished eating you're to get dressed and hurry along to the lounge. You've got a whole morning of lessons before you." And with that she picked up the mugs and empty cinnamon bun plate and left. Schoolwork was the last thing I wanted to do. I dawdled in getting dressed and must have made sure my room was tidy at least a dozen times before leaving my room with my schoolbag and laptop in tow.

*

"What have you got those with you for?" The greeting Rachel gave me as I walked into the living room; it's nine fires already burning brightly, even though it was before nine in the morning. I wondered momentarily if they'd ever gone out.

"I thought you had a morning of lessons planned. That's what Kara said." I was slightly confused. How could I have lessons without my books?

"Oh! I see she forgot to mention what type of lesson. Put those in the kitchen for now. I've got something else planned." Rachel's eyes glinted in the glow from the flames dancing in the various hearths. I hurriedly placed my books and computer in the kitchen and raced back into the living room, curious to find out what sort of lessons I would be having.

On re-entry I discovered that the furniture had been moved to the edges of the circular room and in the middle lay a blanket with a map of the solar system on it. On top of which lay the original chest from our earlier discussions. It was open and minus the photo album. I joined Rachel and we sat down next to the chest. She passed it to me and asked me to remove its contents. As I did so, I laid the items in front of me so I could see them easily. It wasn't until I finished emptying the box that Rachel spoke again.

"Each of these objects belongs to you. They are your birthright and they hold potential powers which when combined with yours will enable you to do more than you ever thought possible. Each item was crafted by Tillie whilst she was carrying you, as is the tradition within our family. All except this one." She picked up a polished stick that was made out of beech and had beautiful carvings etched into its circumference. "This one was made by me as it is right for the matriarch to do." I marvelled at the items my natural mother had undertaken the making of. There was a beautiful garment of a turquoise material with stars embroidered into it, a beautiful double-edged knife about six inches in length with a clear quartz handle, a set of hand-woven baskets, a white handled knife with a curved blade, two wooden bowls, a marble mortar and pestle and a pair of chalices made from steel with beautiful marks scratched into their outer surfaces. I ran my fingers over each item and felt a dramatic surge of power run through my fingertips to the rest of my body. It was unlike anything I had ever experienced. I was connected to them all.

"Before we start unlocking their power, however," Rachel caught my eye with those deep blue pools that sat in her eye sockets, "we need to unlock and train that mind of yours. It will take hard work and dedication and you will need to use every ounce of your mental and physical energy. It won't be an easy task but when you achieve it you will find that your skills will become second nature to you." Hard work? For once a challenge! I knew that it would probably drain me, but it would make a decent change from the boredom of normal lessons and homework!

"Right, let's clear away your tools and begin." I placed them back in the chest, shut the lid and moved it to the edge of the room. "Kneel down in front of me and try to empty your mind of its usual everyday matter. Close your eyes and concentrate purely on your breathing." I did as I was told, listening only to the intake and expulsion of air from my chest and Rachel's voice. I reached a place within me that I had never found before. I discovered that whilst my body remained planted firmly on the blanket, my spirit had soared above the ground and directly opposite me was Rachel's.

"That happened quicker than I would have expected it to. Still you are the prophesised one perhaps that is why. Anyhow, shall we continue? This form of communication is the one way in which we can converse even when asleep. It is the astral plain in which our spirits can wonder freely without fear of persecution. It is one of the best ways of escaping the trials of torture and has served our ancestors on many occasions during which The Sergeant has tried to extract information from them, for although he may have certain powers, his do not extend to the metaphysical plains. From this vantage point we are free to travel through time and space undetected. The only down side is that we must remember to keep an eye on our physical selves to make sure that we are not captured or attacked (something which cannot occur in La Grotte as it is magically sealed) and that we cannot enter areas that The Sergeant has protected with his boundary spells. This is the reason I have not found your parents or Monique yet but there is still hope." I looked down at my body and noticed tears streaming down my face. It appeared that on the astral plain I could feel emotional pain but not express it in the same way as I would ordinarily. Rachel's spirit connected with mine by way of my metaphysical hand and led me out of the room and through the caves of La Grotte. In a second living room Kara and Timothy were playing a game of chess, unaware of our presence. I saw several bathrooms, a large library, a study and many more bedrooms; the network of caverns went on for miles.

*

After returning to the living room Rachel taught me how to will myself back into my body and once my physical and spiritual bodies were reconnected I realised how free I had felt when not confined to the earthly restrictions being fully corporal places on the human spirit. I felt exhausted from the crying fit my physical body had endured when I had left it on the ground, and my spirit was dying to be liberated from the complications of its physical counterpart.

It took several minutes for my two selves to reunite, leaving me more worn out than I ever thought possible.

"It's ok. The first time does tend to take it out of you a bit. You'll get used to the rejoining process in time. However we'll concentrate on unravelling your other abilities before going back to the astral plain. But first a tea break." She went off to the kitchen to put the kettle on. I sat, stunned. It was as if I had been watching everything that had unfolded when I was on the astral plain whilst sitting in the cinema with a movie playing on the big screen. I continued pondering the surreal experience until Rachel re-entered carrying two mugs of peppermint tea. I could have killed for caffeine, the only hot drinks I had had since entering La Grotte were buckets full of herbal tea - in particular peppermint. Rachel picked up on my though train:

"I know you're getting sick of drinking this Lana, but it aids mental abilities and in particular psychic powers. I promise you that when lessons are finished for the day that I will give you a bottle of coke and as much chocolate as you can eat. But for now humour me, allow the tea to help you open your mind." She smiled at me and I found that I couldn't refuse her anything. We sat on one of the couches and quietly consumed the tea. It gave a chance for reflection and also time to contemplate what other lessons were to come.

*

The next lesson was much harder than the first one. It involved blocking Rachel from entering my mind. She called it 'l'empêchment d'esprit' I called it the most annoyingly difficult thing I had ever had to do. I admit that I wanted to be challenged, but the fact that everything that I had ever tried to do before had come so easily meant that I was getting quickly frustrated with my inability in this area and it did not help with my concentration on the task at hand. Which apparently was why Rachel had just delved into the back of my mind and pulled out the memory of me in first year falling over Cassie's foot before her cronies locked me in my own locker. This was driving me mad and I was crying almost constantly with the agony of past occasions of torment from my peers. I wanted it all to stop yet couldn't sever the connection. Wherever I moved in the room my mind was locked with Rachel's the pain was unbearable and I couldn't see any way out. As I despaired I reached the lowest point of the lesson and it was then that it came to me. Physically I could do nothing, but maybe, mentally I could push her out of my head. If I was to visualise Rachel's mind as a physical entity - more specifically, Rachel herself - I may be able to force her out. It took all the physical, emotional and mental strength I had but I could not think of anything else to do. I closed my eyes and fixated on the image of Rachel when I had first seen her, the day our eyes had connected and I raised my metaphysical hands and shoved her with all the energy I could muster. Suddenly, very suddenly in fact, I felt space in my head; it was no longer occupied by two minds. I was exhausted and ready to keel over with the effort but I caught a glimpse of Rachel out of the corner of my eye. She was slumped against the wall in between two fireplaces. I ran across the blanket and rushed to her side. She looked pale and shocked, she wasn't bleeding but I was sure if I had attempted pushing her earlier then she would have been more severely hurt. I had temporarily forgotten that whilst Rachel was in my head she was also still connected to her body and therefore the physical plain. I checked she was breathing and comfortable before attempting something I wasn't sure how to do. I couldn't leave her, I felt, *no* I was responsible for Rachel getting hurt.

"Kara, Tim? Can you hear me?" I waited. Nothing but silence. Something I was doing was wrong. I was mentally projecting but it wasn't getting me anywhere. I scanned the room searching for a clue. Shouting wouldn't work in the cavernous system of the homestead. My voice would echo and therefore the sound would disintegrate. I needed help to communicate with them. Perhaps the astral plain, but that would mean leaving my body and therefore leaving Rachel.

"Kara, Tim? Are you getting this?" Again nothing. This was beginning to become annoying. I scanned the room again, something caught my eye, and it was sticking out from behind the thirty-six hour clock. I was sure that it hadn't been there before. I walked across to the mantelpiece on which it stood and removed the item from behind the clock. It was a notepad-sized book, black in colour and like the books that had come out of the gigantic chest when Rachel had unpacked; it had nothing written on its cover or spine. I took it back over to where Rachel was lying, still unconscious but still breathing. I flicked through its pages and discovered spells and techniques handwritten within its pages. Wishing there was a reference page, I skimmed the titles on each page and found what I was looking for. It was a page entitled 'La Communication Télépathique' it contained step-by-step instructions for different scenarios but none applied to the working of the telepathic wavelengths within La Grotte. I studied the page over and over it was an absolute nightmare. How could I reach them? As I was pondering the problem, Kara and Tim their heads out of the left-hand corridor.

"You called?"

"Yeah, but I thought…"

"We heard you but not clearly, we thought maybe it was just thought static from your lessons." Tim smiled at me and for the first time I saw Rachel in him.

"Guess not though by the looks of

Maman." Kara walked over to where Rachel lay with a sofa cushion under her head.

"Let me guess, you pushed her out of your mind?"

"Well yeah, how did you...?"

"I did it when she was teaching me l'empêchment d'esprit. Don't worry she'll come round in a minute. She really should have remembered to guard herself. But then you were doing things the right way. If you'd have done it earlier she'd probably still be conscious although just as bruised. You see the further someone enters a mind, the more they lose the connection with their body."

"Maybe she did expect me to do it earlier, I managed astral projection quicker than she thought I would. I suck at this." I slumped into a chair and burst into loud sobs.

"It's not your fault Lana. Astral is easier as it requires a relaxed state of mind. It was the first time in a while your brain could shut off the stresses its been dealing with. L'empêchment requires a lot of concentration and your mind would have clogged with your worst memories and fears as you tried to focus." Tim gave me a hug and went off to the kitchen.

"Perhaps we should stop for today. We both need to rest." Rachel had come round. I hadn't killed her! It was an irrational thought but I was just so relieved.

"But I… I want to continue. I'm sorry I hurt you. We can try one more time."

"Not at the moment. We should rest until tomorrow. You've been through a big ordeal, I pulled up memories that you need to lay to rest and my backs killing me." At that moment, Tim returned with steaming mugs of hot chocolate and a tray of chocolate muffins. Perhaps stopping was a good idea after all, it meant proper food.

*

That night we sat around the kitchen table discussing the experiences we had all had when learning to tame various psychic skills. Apparently Timothy had taken three weeks to master astral projection and it had taken Rachel an hour and a half to get him to rejoin his body. He had been so pleased at achieving it that his spirit had not wanted to join the physical plain again. Kara told me how when she had finally pushed her mother from her mind she had knocked Rachel out so badly that she had considered calling an ambulance. Rachel had not come round for four and a half hours. It was amazing to hear my aunt and uncle talk of their experiences. In a way it calmed my nerves. They told me of the lessons to come and the pitfalls behind them. How when Tillie had been learning to communicate telepathically she had accidentally broadcast her and Rachel's thoughts to everyone in the house and the surrounding area. Some poor farmer ploughing a nearby field was convinced he had heard the voice of God. I was bound to make mistakes in learning to control my skills. I wasn't after all trying my hand at a new language or learning the piano - those were skills that had to be taught. I was learning to use something that I had been born with and that required a different training tactic. I felt so good as I drank my last mug of hot chocolate and was dragging my feet when it came to bedtime. But both my aunt and uncle and my grandmother insisted that I go. It was with some reluctance that I finally went to bed at a quarter to midnight.

I lay in bed unable to sleep. My mind was racing with the aftermath of the day's lessons and with the conversation at the kitchen table. I was finally a part of something that meant I wasn't odd or skirting the edge of. It was great. I shut my eyes and sent goodnight messages telepathically to my family and received messages back just as quickly. But there was an extra message delivered with the others. A voice I intrinsically knew, however, I couldn't believe I was hearing it. I sent a thought back, one I was sure would be futile, the fourth voice was imagined, I was sure of it.

'Maman, c'est vous?'

'Oui mon enfant. I heard your call.'

'But how, you're not in La Grotte and I thought that it was sealed from the outside world!' I was flabbergasted. I was having a conversation with my birth mother!

'I am not outside; I was just waiting for the right moment. You and your Mémé bypassed my room when you were on the astral plain. I did not want you to know that I was there. I needed to let you grow, let you discover who you are before I entered your world. I will see you tomorrow my daughter.'

'No, Maman, I want to see you now. I
need to see you now. I'm ready to see you.'
I couldn't believe she was holding off seeing
me and wanted me to do the same. I wanted
her to take over my lessons. I wanted
something I hadn't had in fourteen and a half
years and I wanted it now.

'Wait until tomorrow, it will give you time
to adjust, it'll give me time to adjust.' I heard
the thought, but it was too late. I used my
persipacité sixiéme to find her. I walked
down the tunnel, past Rachel's room, past
the Tim and Kara's rooms, through the
second lounge and down another corridor to
her room. I stood at the door, trepidation
running through my smaller than average
body. But I had to do it. I knocked and
waited. I was petrified.

"I knew you couldn't hold it off. You're
just like I was at your age, stubborn." For a
moment I thought it was just another
received thought. But no Maman was
standing in front of me. I couldn't believe it.
Swap my blond hair for brown and she and I
were the double of each other. She led me
into her room, which was lined with photos
of me. Ones that had obviously been passed

on by Mum and Dad, there were photos from every year of my life, she'd even framed one of me potty training. It was weird to think that whilst she had kept an eye on me from afar I hadn't even had one photograph until Rachel had given me the photo album to look at.

"Sit, sit. Let me get a proper look at you. I've been longing for this moment ever since we handed you over to the Le Monniers. You're so beautiful. Je t'aime avec tout mon coeur ma fille. I always have done and always will."

"I missed having you in my life Maman. I'm glad you're here with me. I just cannot believe I'm sitting here with you." Tears welled up in my eyes, the rush of emotion was immensely overpowering.

"I know my child, I know. But I am here and so are you of that you can be sure. However, I think that maybe for now we should go to sleep. I'm not sending you back to your room. There's enough space on the bed for both of us." She'd picked up on the way I was feeling. There was no way I would have gone back down the two corridors to my room. Not now. She was the person I had always wanted to be with.

And so that night I fell asleep in the arms of Maman. We were together again.

CHAPTER FIVE

Mothers and Daughters

Mémé, sorry Rachel, had the shock of her life when Maman and I walked into the kitchen together the following morning. The fact that the frying pan missed her foot by half an inch was testament to her disbelief. To this day I don't think she would be able to miss with such accuracy if you asked her. The poor woman wasn't so lucky with the eggs and bacon however. The eggs stuck sunny side down to the ceiling and the bacon managed to lodge itself behind one of the torches on wall. Needless to say, for days afterwards we had to dodge the egg yolk waterfall in the kitchen.

"Tillie je pense que…"

"Je sais Maman but I decided that the time was right. I trusted my instincts as a mother and they told me that I needed to break my silence. I decided to communicate." Thank La Mére Eternelle! Mémé was going to direct the assault at Maman; there was no way this could be aimed at me.

"Mathilde! You should have consulted me first! I know I taught you to trust your persipacité sixiéme but still did you think what consequences it could have had on Lana's learning and that it may cloud her judgement of things? You are just as stubborn and reckless as when you were a teenager!" Her voice lowered and she stared fixatedly at Maman. I thought that she was about to blow a gasket.

"Maman, no offence intended but this matter is between me and my daughter not me and you or Lana and you. I felt that she needed me and that is what helped me make the decision. Whilst she may not have showed it to you, deep down she was crying for the love and attention that only I could give." Maman why did you have to go and bring me into it? I did not see how that was going to help things.

"I see… so you're questioning the way in which I run the household and family as is my right to do. I have taken on the role handed down to me by my mother and you dare to think that you are ready for such a position? You are still infantile in your approach to life Mathilde and until you reach your third tri-decade I do not see you having the power to challenge my role!" If possible her voice had gone quieter than a whisper yet she had not yet reverted to telepathic conversation.

"Maman that is not what I meant... I would never challenge you, vous êtes la matrone. You have control that is how it should be. I merely meant to suggest that as Lana's mother I should have a larger input into the way in which her life with us is led. I feel that she needs more than a matriarchal figure she needs her Maman." Unlike Mémé, Maman was beginning to raise her voice and the way in which she was clenching her fists reminded me of myself when I was feeling angry or frustrated.

"Lana," the sound of my name made me jump. "Is it true? Did you feel the need for Mathilde to be with you?" Oh crap! I had been pulled in and couldn't very well turn around and say nothing.

"Rachel... Mémé... I... I love you

dearly and am grateful for all you have done so far and will do for me in the future but there is a bond between mother and daughter that can be simulated but not emulated. It is this bond that I have craved since I found out that I was adopted and only Maman can fill the void the lack of that bond created. I am sure that you understand, for you have that same bond with Maman." I stood waiting for a scathing reply that would tear my skin with whip strokes.

"I see. Thank you for your honesty Lana. I can see that you have thought deeply about this and respect that you replied frankly with no sense of rebellion in your attitude towards the situation. Without meaning to upset Tillie," she glanced at her daughter, "this is where you two differ. You have the ability to control your anger beyond your years, although hormones do interfere with your rationality at points. This occasional lack of clarity is due to your age and something that given a few years I have no doubt you will grow out of."

"Thank you Mémé. May I ask you for a favour? As much as I know my schooling is important to the cause that I will one day have to fight for, I would like to spend today getting to know Maman so that I may continue with my studies having cleared my mind of the many questions I have swimming in my head." It wasn't going to work, I knew it. Mémé would prefer for me to continue straight away, her furrowed brow told me so. As much as I wanted to hear what she was thinking, a telepathic link would have been an invasion of privacy. The minutes ticked by and I could see that she was wrestling with the two halves of her brain.

"I suppose that one or two days rest wouldn't hurt and it would help you to focus when you're studying. Yes ok, favour granted."

*

It was after breakfast that Maman and I went for a walk through La Grotte to an area that I had not yet entered. There at the end of the bedroom tunnel lay a subterranean garden. It was the most magical thing I had seen so far in the system of underground chambers that had now become my home, my safe haven, my world.

There were rose bushes, a couple of apple trees, beautiful and varying plants of all descriptions and underneath the tallest apple tree on a beautifully manicured lawn lay an ornately carved wooden bench. We sat and for a while just looked at each other. There was no need for speech and yet there was. The question of who should begin was playing heavily on my mind and by the look of Maman's thoughtful eyes it was on hers too. It wasn't an awkward silence don't get me wrong. It was just that well not only did I know if I should be starting the conversation but how to start it. I had what I wanted the time to ask my mother to fill me in on everything I needed to know and yet I couldn't phrase the thoughts in such a way as to make them coherent when they left my mouth. Instead I sat and enjoyed the view of the artificially sunlit plants and the smell of Maman's perfume. The fragrance was intoxicating and stirred a long lost feeling of safety and being wanted. I knew that I had been safe and wanted with Mum and Dad but this was different. It was an infantile security that felt more natural than anything in my life ever had. I gently leaned in to Maman and slowly shut my eyes.

Conversation could wait until later, I had my mother and whilst I knew I should be talking I was too busy enjoying myself.

*

By lunchtime I had gotten nowhere near to discussing the thing that was really playing on my mind - my biological father. Or as Mémé had called him when I happened to eavesdrop on a conversation she had been having with Kara on the first night in La Grotte - my sperm donor. She obviously hated him, and I was curious to know why. I broached the subject as Maman and I made salad for the family.

"Maman, I have something I want to ask."

"Go ahead ma fille. I'll answer anything that is in my power to."

"Who's my biological father and why does Mémé hate him so much?"

"I knew we'd get round to that and some point. I just thought it might be a bit later. I should have expected you to be just as inquisitive as me." She looked at me with slight amusement. "You're father was a local lad who went to the all boys school down the road from yours. I fell in love with him from the moment I saw him. His name was William and he was tall, dark and handsome. We started dating when we were fourteen. Maman wasn't too bothered at first, I guess she thought it was nothing more than a teenage romance and wouldn't last very long. She was content in believing that it would be over in a couple of weeks. However, it lasted for four months. In the third month we slept together and that's when it all started to go wrong. Maman found out and went ballistic. Apparently she felt that he had defiled her baby and she ordered us to stop seeing each other. We kept seeing each other in secret; Monique, Kara and Tim helped me to keep the secret by covering for me. Then the day after we celebrated our fourth month anniversary, Kara was giving me my usual spiritual health check - your aunt is especially gifted with healing powers - when she discovered that I wasn't alone. She found another life force combined with mine, yours. I told William about you the next day. He blanched and told me that he was not ready to be a father and if I ever told anyone you were his, he would deny everything. I came home in tears. Maman was furious because I'd lost my virginity and because William had effectively disowned me. She couldn't make up her mind as to whether or not she should be yelling at him or me. I went to my room that night feeling scared and worried. I was a young girl who in nine months would be a mother. I wasn't sure what to do. I went to school the next day and everybody was pointing and laughing. Apparently William had told them that I had gotten pregnant by someone else and had tried to blame you on him. I ran out of school and got a bus straight home. Maman was furious she marched round to the boys school and had a go at William and when she came back told me that she would be home schooling me. I was so ashamed of the situation in which I found myself. For an instant I considered a termination. Only an instant, but your spirit spoke to me and I realised that I could never do it. You were and still are my baby. Giving you up was the hardest thing that I ever had to do." She finished putting salad on Mémé's plate and looked at me. She seemed scared to say anything else. Scared that because I knew she had considered an abortion that I wouldn't love her. I showed her she was wrong. I put the tray with the drinks on it onto the table and hugged her with all my might. Maman had told me the truth and I valued her more for it. I couldn't believe that my father - no my sperm donor - could have been so cruel. The man I had always wanted to know no longer held my respect and there was no way I ever wanted to meet him. I already had a father, one who needed my biological family and me more than ever.

*

Life seemed strained to say the least over the next few days. Maman and Mémé argued and argued. Mémé was furious that Maman had dared mentioned William to me and Maman hated the fact that Mémé wasn't giving her more freedom. My lessons had temporarily stopped and I quickly ran out of schoolwork to take my mind off the rows. Instead I holed myself up in the library or the study reading the black bound volumes that seemed to cover the four hundred library and study shelves. Each seemed to be full of spells and lessons on controlling telepathic and healing powers. As much as I wished I was learning from Maman and Mémé I found it easier to study away from them out of the books. It was peaceful in the two rooms and I could concentrate on learning and controlling the skills I would have acquired under my family's tutelage. Thank goodness for the network of caves! Being in a house would have meant that I wouldn't have been able to escape the arguments. When Mum had argued with the twins, the house had vibrated with the volume and even my music couldn't drown it out. I picked up tips on telepathic communication and blocking, learnt how to astral project and allow myself to watch my physical body from wherever I was - it involved dividing my spiritual entity in such a way that the two halves remained connected but could separate so I could watch both my body and the scene I had arrived at simultaneously. It was a difficult process to master but meant that I could make sure that Maman and Mémé were not tearing each other apart and that Kara and Timothy were not plunged in between them trying to keep the peace. They talked so rapidly in French that it sounded like two bees buzzing more than actual speech. Kara regularly brought me drinks and food. She hated the fact that I had locked myself away but understood my reasons. Occasionally she or Tim would come in and help me with my studies but most of the time I was left to my own devices. I liked it that way. It meant I could concentrate more readily.

It was the fourth day after the arguments had begun and I found myself in the library yet again. They had been at it all night and I had barely slept. It was like Mémé truly hated Maman. She was always having a go at her and if I wasn't mistaken had told her the only reason she hadn't kicked her out of La Grotte was because I wanted her there. I was angry and hurting I wanted nothing more than for them to stop and make up. It was this anger that revealed a power I was not aware I had. I was so angry that I had stopped studying and was pacing the room trying to calm myself down and work out a way of resolving the situation. As I walked towards the desk for the fourth time, I had a loud clatter behind me. Eight books from the shelves two feet to my right had fallen onto the floor. I picked them back up and resumed my pacing. On my way back to the desk, a new set of books did the same. I stared in disbelief. If it had been the same set I would have thought that the shelf was wonky but how could it be? These new books came from a shelf three shelves up from the last lot. I paused for a moment and picked up the volume I had been studying. I flicked through its yellow pages and quickly came across what I had been looking for - telekinesis - the power to move objects with the mind. The page, which contained the information, was entitled 'La Mouvement d'Objets Avec l'Esprit'. It detailed how, in rare cases, telekinesis had been discovered in various Magiques who had suffered great pressure. It was an unusual gift that surfaced once every ten generations - guess it was my turn. According to the book, the power usually foretold of a great Magique, usually female, on whom it would fall to protect the family in some way or another and that the ability was the hardest of all powers to control. I was determined to control the power; after all I already knew that I was meant to protect the family and the other inhabitants of Laterrétoile at some point in my future. This was one power no-one else would have been able to show me how to use and that meant I had an excuse to stay away from the arguments that bit longer. From that moment on I devoted all my time to mastering my newfound skill. It was a hard and arduous road. You know how you feel when everyone else in class catches on quicker than you or someone learns how to play a sport or instrument before you and even though you try you still find yourself failing? That's how I felt, but I had no one to compete with except myself. I'd get up at half five, have my shower and fit in two hours work before breakfast and wouldn't leave the library or study until gone midnight. In fact, on several occasions I worked so late that Kara found me sitting on a chair with my head on a desk, snoring. In the end she put a foldout bed in each room so that I did not have to risk waking everyone up by walking down corridors at three a.m. It took three weeks to make any real progress and by that time I had amassed about twelve hours sleep during the entire study period and the arguments, unbeknown to be and stopped. It was six-thirty on a Sunday morning and I was tired having not yet been to bed. I was about to crawl into the camp bed and get a catnap when I found myself wishing that I could just bring the bed to me rather than walk to it. At first I though I was dreaming and rubbed my eyes in disbelief. The bed lifted off of the floor and gently sat itself down beside me. I was shocked. I'd achieved what I was beginning to think was the impossible. I had controlled my power. To prove I hadn't imagined the whole thing, I sat on the bed and looked at the study desk and concentrated on the lamp that sat on its right-hand corner. I willed it to move six inches to the left using what little energy I had left. At first it sat perfectly still, then slowly it began to shake and then suddenly it rose into the air and moved exactly six inches to the left of where it sat. I had done it! I had conquered telekinesis! I lay down and shut my eyes, falling asleep instantly.

*

I walked into the lounge for the first time since the arguments had begun and sat quietly down in one of the armchairs. I had decided to mention nothing of my new power until I was sure that Maman and

Mémé had settled their differences. I also thought that it might be more fun to show them as opposed to tell them. I sat watching the fire and contemplated how yesterday I had managed to control one of the most difficult inborn abilities known to our kind in three weeks. According to the book it usually took years of practice. It was still early and I knew that the other family members would not stir for at least and hour. I rested my head against the arm and fell into a deep sleep. When I came round Maman smiled down at me.

"Hello sleepy-head. I was going to wake you but thought better of it. You must have been exhausted."

"What time is it?"

"A little after midday."

"Oh!" I couldn't believe I had slept for six hours without being woken by the noise of the rest of the family. Mémé came bustling in with a tray of hot croissants and mugs of steaming, regular tea.

"You're awake! Thought you might come round soon. Glad you joined us, we haven't seen you for ages." She smiled gently.

"Well I hate to sound rude, but I

couldn't stand the arguments. You two were driving me mad!" I stared up guiltily.

"I can understand that. But we stopped arguing about a week ago. Kara should have told you. She said you'd been studying on your own day and night. It must have been tough going for you. You hardly had any advice. I'm sorry."

"Me too. We should never have made you feel so uncomfortable. Can you forgive us ma fille?" Maman looked horrified at the fact she may have let me down.

"Of course I forgive you." They were family and family means unconditional love and forgiveness in my book. "Can I show you guys something?" I was sure they were ok with each other and this was important to me.

"Sure." Mémé looked curious.

"Put that tray on the table over there. That's it. Now watch." Before their eyes I moved the tray and its contents without spilling a thing from one side of the room to the other. Maman gasped and Mémé collapsed into a nearby chair. By the looks on their faces, neither one could believe it.

"Do that again." Maman definitely

couldn't believe it. So I did. I moved the tray back to the original table upon which it had been placed.

"That would usually take years of study and by the looks of it you've accomplished in a matter of weeks what other Magiques, like myself have never managed to accomplish. You truly are the prophesised one." Mémé almost fell prostrate on the floor with humility. I could have laughed myself stupid if it wasn't for the fact that I did not want to hurt her feelings.

The fact that I had shown such power led to a drastic changes in the household. Tim and Kara were treating me like an elder. They refused to let me help with general household chores, which was driving me insane. Maman and Mémé decided that it was useless teaching me anything as I could pick it up from the volumes in the study and library easily enough. Instead they presented me with my own volume. It's pages were blank so that I could fill it with my own thoughts, incantations and information I had gathered that I felt relevant to pass on to any children I may have in the future. Along with the book I was given new pens, pencils, pencil colours, paints and felt tips. Each to be used only in the books - tools to create my legacy. I spent weeks carefully rough drafting on school notepads and then copying into my new book. It was important to me that what I put into it was written in a way which future generations would understand and utilise it. The easiest part was translating my thoughts into French, the primary language of my natal family. The hardest was the illustrations. I had to carefully decide how to present the book in an intriguing and attractive manner that would reach its audience. It had to be highly personal as any form of journal always is, but at the same time not too personal to make anyone reading it feel as if they were intruding. It was the sort of challenge I enjoy.

*

It was while I was putting the finishing touches to my astral projection pages that I heard a strange muffled noise from the study. I grabbed a torch from one of the brackets on the library wall and headed across the corridor to the study. I pushed open the door slightly afraid of what I might meet as I knew the others were in bed because as usual I had been working well into the night. I put the torch in ahead of me and then poked my head round the door. At first all I saw was the dark shell of the study, it's torches having been extinguished by Kara when she had gone to bed several hours before. But I could still hear the muffled noise. It sounded like someone crying. As I edged my way round the room towards the desk where the sound seemed to be coming from I lit a few of the other torches with my own and placed mine in an empty bracket. I have always been a bit afraid of the dark, and the light quelled my fears somewhat. I approached the desk and peered over it, eager to see who or what was sobbing their heart out behind its oak structure. I could have collapsed; there behind the desk was the last person I expected to see.

"I need to see Maman and Lana."

CHAPTER SIX

Monique

I was a little shocked to say the least when I realised that Monique was the person crouched behind the desk. I instantly wanted to curse her into oblivion but knew from my studies that by the universal power of three I would suffer large consequences. Instead I sent a message to Mémé by way of my mind and prayed that it would not wake the others. I begged her to come to my aid and she arrived quicker than I thought possible. She came into the study, her long hair flowing in bits from the bun she had obviously forgotten to take out before going to bed. Her dressing gown was open, barely covering her pyjamas. Mémé looked rather flustered to say the least.

"Where is she?"

"Behind the desk. She wants to talk to us. By the way she keeps looking around, I don't think that she knows where she is or how she got here. She keeps crying and mumbling. I can't get any sense out of her."

"Ok Lana. Fetch your mother and the others. Take them directly to the primary living room. We're going to need everyone for this. Drag Timothy out of bed if you have to. He can be such a lazy git. Don't tell them what has happened just tell them its an emergency - hurry."

I did exactly as I was told and hurried down the corridors, through the second living room and into the bedroom corridor. I burst into Kara's room and shook her awake. Quickly explained and asked her to wake Tim whilst I went and got Maman. We met in the lounge ten minutes later. Mémé and Monique were already there. It took a while for everyone in the room to adjust to Monique sitting there. Maman kept eyeing her as if she was a ticking time bomb waiting to explode. Kara sat there absent mindedly chewing her nails and staring at Monique with curiosity. Tim on the other hand sat looking fixatedly at one of the fires.

Like me, he couldn't bring himself to look at the traitor cradled in Mémé's arms. She had kidnapped my parents, the ones I had called Mum and Dad since I started talking at four months old and now Mémé was treating her like a precious toy doll. Protecting her from the rest of us as if she were the victim in this situation. The anger inside of me was reaching boiling point and the only way I could stop myself from launching at her was to project my anger onto the nearest sofa cushion. I began pummelling it so hard that feathers started to fly and Maman had to tear herself away from her twin and take it from my hands.

"Timothy, Kara, Tillie, stay here with your sister. Make sure she is comfortable and stays put. Lana come with me." Mémé had regained some of her normal composure and had taken charge once more.

"No. I will not leave my biological family to be torn out form underneath me by the same person who took my adoptive parents! I'm staying put."

"Lana you will do as you are told. Monique is in no fit state to attempt such a feat and you forget that they can easily look after themselves, they have the gifts of our ancestors."

"But she has The Sergeant's borrowed power. She can easily…"

"She cannot. You forget that he cannot penetrate La Grotte. It is sealed with impenetrable magic. Come." I gave Maman one fleeting last look and was swept out of the room quicker than my feet could carry me. It was obvious that Mémé was in a hurry to get to where we were going.

*

We reached the library with such speed that the journey was and still is a blur. Mémé grabbed a large purple covered volume from the top shelf of one of the bookcases and then grabbed a trunk from under one of the desks. She pulled a key out of her dressing gown and unlocked the trunk. Then she ordered me to run and get the chest containing my magical tolls from my room. I fled as quick as my legs could carry me without thinking and within a minute was back in the library. Mémé had already started pulling things from the locked trunk, including a smaller version of the universe blanket. I couldn't understand

what was so important. My head was still
fogged by rage and confusion at Monique's
presence for me to think clearly. She must
have sensed it because Mémé told me to
clear my head. We had to work fast if we
were going to save Monique and find out
what she had to say. Saving her was the last
thing on my mind, admittedly I wished she
was dead, but told myself that Mémé knew
what she was doing and that I should go
along with her. She placed five bowls at
different points on the blanket, grabbed
various sachets of herbs and told me to
empty my chest. I did so and she instructed
me to bring over my mortar and pestle and
the highly polished engraved stick. She then
told me to sit and grabbed the book from the
desk. What she did next was something I
had read about but not yet put into practice.
She walked to each of the bowls making the
shape of a star and chanting a summoning
incantation, one that called for La Mére
Eternelle to bless the star and help us with
our workings. She then returned to the
centre of the star and took up a sachet of
allspice and asked me to empty it into my
mortar. Then she passed me basil, a bay leaf,
some blackberries, a carnation flower and

some crushed thyme. She asked me to grind them together as she chanted a different incantation:

"La Mére Eternelle écoutez de notre prière. S'engage nous avec votre présence.

(Hear our prayer Eternal Mother. Engage us with your presence)

Nous faisons cet charme pour Soleil Monique Cornique pour que nous rendons son esprit et ses facultés mentale.

(We cast this spell for Monique Soleil Cornique so that we can restore her spirit and mind.)

Nous demande á vous de une béndédiction sur cet charme pour que c'est possible pour il de travaillerara son emploi.

(We request that you bless this working so that it may do its job.)

Merci beaucoup pour votre patience, nous sommes blessé par votre présence.

(Thank you for patience, we have been blessed by your presence)

Nous prions que cet charme en rendre le santé a notre membre de famille, comme les pouvoirs curatifs de la lune de Laterrétoile et les grains de sable sur les plages de notre patrie.

(We pray that this spell will return the health of our family member like the healing powers of

the moon of Laterrétoile and the grains of sand on
the beaches of our home planet.)

Aussi que les charmes des Ancêtres.
(Like the spells of the Ancestors.)

She closed the star with another charm as I laid down the pulp, which was now contained within my mortar. When the star was closed we cleared up everything except the pestle and then carried it through to the primary lounge. The mixture of different aromas was overpowering to say the least. We entered the room and found that Timothy was now standing by the stairwell still unable to look at his sister, Kara was sitting with Monique and Maman hadn't moved at all since we had left. Mémé hurried to the kitchen coming back minutes later with a mug of hot water and a teaspoon.

Lana mix in a couple of spoonfuls of the potion with the hot water." I did as told, not wanting to upset the apple cart but still unsure of what help the potion could be. I finished and handed it over to Mémé who had taken over Kara's position next to Monique.

"Monique, c'est Maman. I want you

to drink some of this, it'll help you to think more clearly and calm down. It'll help you understand what is going on around you." Monique did as she was told and the rest of us just waited. It took about half an hour for the potion to kick in and my anger had started to boil again. I really couldn't see the point of it at all. As far as I was concerned she was a traitor and deserved to be locked up.

"Maman? Tim? Kara? Tillie? Lana? Thank la Mére Eternelle that you're all well. I've been trying to find you all for months." Yeah right, talk about trying to soften us up.

"Where have you been Monique? You were last seen at the Le Monnier house and then both you and Gwen and Jack disappeared. Then I found that mirror in your room. I just cannot believe that you're in league with him!"

"I'm not Maman, I swear it."

"Then tell us why you kidnapped my parents you traitor!" I was fuming, she was spinning lies to try and protect herself I knew it.

"Lana, I am sorry that your parents have been taken but it wasn't me that did it. If you'll let me, I'll explain things as best I can." Why should I let her? Mémé gave me a stern look.

"Go on then, prove your innocence."

"About eight months ago I had gone into town to get some supplies. I was running out of Belladonna and various other ingredients and I wanted a new scrying crystal. I was in Wicraze, you know, the apothecary and crystal store in the market. I was searching for the right crystal and this man walked in. He came over to me and introduced himself as Jacques. I told him that I was rather busy and didn't really have time to talk to him. He was quite persistent, he wanted to go for coffee and I refused. Jacques was threatening to get physical, and the shop owner who had been watching the whole thing asked him to leave before she called the police. He did so reluctantly hissing something I couldn't quite catch. I pushed him from my mind and bought my list of shopping. After leaving the shop I decided it was time for lunch and headed to the café down the alley next to the market. I ordered my usual and as soon as it arrived I tucked in. I wanted to get home by three o'clock to help Maman with the Saturday evening meal. It was as I was half way through my ham and cucumber sandwich that Jacques turned up. I had the feeling that he'd been following me, and before I could protect myself he had made his way over to the table at which I was sitting. Something was wrong with the way he smiled at me. He did not seem the same as he had in Wicraze. In fact I could have sworn that he was a completely different person. Don't get me wrong, it wasn't like I had wanted anything to do with him on our first meeting, in fact he had scared me quite considerably, it was just that his aura had changed and he seemed more determined. He told me that I was to come with him and resistance would be useless. I told him that I thought otherwise and that there was no way I would be going anywhere with him. I was beginning to wish that I had never left the house and I still feel that way now. He pointed a wand at me and told me not to be foolish; The Sergeant would not allow me to slip away. I tried to bolt out of the place but found my feet would not move. I was paralysed - he had performed the *immobiliser* spell on me. Or so I thought. As you know there is a simple charm to remove it, one that can be chanted silently but it did not work.

Jacques was able to control my movements and he took me out of the café and we walked down the street. All the time his wand was pointed at my back and he kept muttering in my ear that I should know better than to argue with the most powerful agent of The Sergeant. It was then I realised who Jacques was. My captor was the one person we have always feared almost as much as his master - Caporal Jacques Le Selleur - head of The Sergeant's forces."

"Oh please! Caporal Le Selleur in the middle of St. Helier you must think we're completely barmy!" I couldn't believe that she was spinning this web of lies. It was obvious to me that she was trying to place the blame on something else. Monique was the one who had kidnapped my parents not Le Selleur.

"Lana give her a chance to finish her story. It's highly possible that they may have found our whereabouts. After all two hundred years of successful hiding was bound to be broken at some time. We were lucky it lasted so long." Mémé was as usual being the voice of reason. Yet I could not help but feel that she was longing for Monique's story to be true.

"If I don't hear anything recognisable as proof within the next fifteen minutes I'm leaving. But I will stay for those fifteen minutes. Convince me Monique."

"Lana, I know you're angry but you have to believe me." She seemed desperate - not to convince me but to gain my trust. "Le Selleur pushed me through town and into a car parked in Minden Place car park. He forced me into the car and drove off. We headed out of town and drove for ages before stopping along the Five Mile road. He had me at wand point the entire time." She burst into sobs, and I felt myself drawn towards the weeping women against my better judgement. "He looked furtively around, making sure we were completely alone and muttered something under his breath. The nest thing I knew, I wasn't in the car, but strapped into a chair in one of The Sergeant's ships. I was bound by magic; the more I struggled the tighter I found myself secured. Le Selleur's glamour disappeared and before me was the aged face of one of the men I have feared the most since childhood. His grey eyes were sunk deep into a gaunt face that was nothing more than skin and bones. Maman he was horrible."

She shuddered at the thought of the sight of him. "He looked at me and laughed, a deep mocking laugh. He called over a group of men who had been out of my sight range and told them to get on with their task. They forced some sort of sleeping draught down my throat and when I woke again I was staring into my own face. The experience wasn't entirely new to me, after all waking up and seeing Tillie's face throughout my childhood was like looking at myself, but this was different. This *was* my face. The woman in front of me was identical to me in every way, right down to the mole on my lip. She had one major difference though. She lacked a soul. Behind her eyes there was nothing. The eyes show the soul, and hers showed a blank void. In my semi-groggy state I couldn't understand why they had made another me. It wasn't until later when they locked me in a cell that I realised. In front of me was a screen showing my double taking my place at home, living my life. They had placed my clone with you so that she could discover the whereabouts of Lana. They succeeded and if it hadn't been for her answering the door to you Maman then she would be with her adoptive parents right now." She paused, stopping only to drink the last dregs of the potion we had brewed. "When the double returned with Gwen and Jack instead of Lana, Le Selleur was fuming. He locked her in my cell. He knew that because of the slip up you would be on to him and he couldn't send the double down again. It took me time to work out how I could work this to my advantage. I was weak through lack of food and the beatings I had been given by the guards when they felt like having fun, and my mind was not at its usual level of keenness. I took my opportunity when the guards came with our rations. Using astral projection I managed to control my body and create the illusion of having no soul behind the eyes. I requested an interview with Le Selleur; I told them that I wanted a second chance to retrieve Lana. He agreed to my request and half an hour later I found myself standing in front of him, my metaphysical body looking down on my physical one. I was sure it wasn't going to work as I had only managed control of my physical body by way of the astral plain once before and if I slipped up he would be sure to notice. I was lucky that it did not happen. He listened to my case carefully and stared intently into my eyes the entire time. He seemed convinced that I was the double and after some consideration allowed me the chance. Le Selleur seemed convinced that I would be allowed back into the family fold and that I could recapture Lana. I counted on him not knowing that as soon as I came within a mile of La Grotte he would no longer be able to trace my energy and that I would be safe. He had me dropped ten seconds away from the boundary and I made my way straight here. Maman I am so sorry. I should have stayed at home that day. Lana please believe that I did not intend for this to happen. It wasn't me who did those awful things." She was exhausted from recounting the tale and whilst I still held onto my suspicions I felt them ebbing from my mind.

"Monique, if that's the case then you can help me find my parents. You have seen the place where they are being held."

"Lana I will help find them by all means and give you any information that comes to mind. But I cannot guarantee that it will help, I so not know the exact whereabouts of the ship." Again she burst into tears. One thing was for sure, the

Monique I had seen at my adoptive parents house had not had the capability of sadness or regret. It was quite possible that she was telling the truth. It all seemed so farfetched that it might be real, yet I couldn't quite lose the slowly lessening doubts.

*

That night I slept in Maman's room. Slept perhaps isn't quite the right word. Maman was tossing and turning and I just couldn't quite get to sleep because of the new information my brain was trying to cope with. We had all gone back to bed on Mémé's orders and when we had left the living room it was nearly six a.m. I was well past the point of tired and as I had done on previous occasions before my life in La Grotte was ready to stay awake for more than twenty-four continuous hours. Yet perhaps I was wrong. After three hours of lying awake staring into the darkness, my body took control of my brain and I fell into a troubled sleep.

*

I woke at around midday; aware of the lack of proper rest I had gotten during my three-hour catnap. Yet try as I might I couldn't go back to the world of unconsciousness that I ached for. My mind was instantly swimming in the tale Monique had told the night before. It seemed confused and bits and pieces kept surfacing in an incomprehensible fashion. I needed food and a cup of peppermint tea to settle my stomach and help clear the thought pathways that had become so intertwined within my mind. I snuck out of the room, not wanting to wake Maman and crept towards the kitchen. I did not want to wake anyone who may still be sleeping. The torches still burnt brightly in their brackets as I wound my way down the corridor towards the first living room and the kitchen, Mémé had obviously forgotten to extinguish them before she had gone to bed. They were comforting in the continuous darkness of underground life, but I longed for the purity of the sun above, the rain which hammered the roof of La Grotte occasionally would have been nice to see, I wanted to feel the wind whistle through my hair, hear the calls of nature again, see my

brothers and sister. For an impulsive
moment I thought about going up the
winding staircase to the outside world and
running free - The Sergeant's detectors
couldn't pick me up with a mile's radius.
But no, if an agent saw me, I would be
captured, it wasn't safe. Instead, after
getting my breakfast, I made my way to the
subterranean garden with the plan to sit and
eat, enjoying the artificial weather and the
feel of actual grass beneath my bare feet.

When I got there however, I found Mémé
still in her silk pyjamas, dressing gown
around her shoulders, her hair barely within
the confines of the bun of the previous day.
It was obvious that she hadn't slept. She was
sitting on the bench that I had sat on with
Maman all those weeks before. At first
Mémé didn't notice me, she seemed to be
offering up a prayer to La Mére Eternelle for
guidance. I know I have said she looked old
when Mum and Dad disappeared but today
she looked ancient. The bags under her eyes
were deep purple and I noticed lines that I
could have sworn were not there before I
went to bed. She looked more like the
biological grandparents of my adoptive

siblings. For the first time in the months that we had spent reunited as granddaughter and grandmother she appeared frail and vulnerable.

"Mémé?"

"Lana, I… I didn't see you there." Mémé's eyes were filled with tears, her hand shaking as she reached out beckoning me forward.

"Mémé, she was telling the truth wasn't she? Monique, I mean."

"I believe so my darling, I believe so." Yet did she? There was something troubling her, the soul within was trying to communicate something that Mémé was finding difficult to communicate.

"Mémé do you feel able to astral? It may help us talk. I know it seems a peculiar request, but our physical bodies are tired and it will take more out of us to communicate on the physical plain." She seemed slightly taken aback by my forwardness, but she agreed. Within moments we were free of our bodies and our metaphysical selves were floating above the ground. The freedom of physical emotion was immense. Mémé looked at me and I realised why she always seemed so youthful - her astral form was a much younger self -

her spirit, lacking the pull of gravity showed the normal picture I saw, one of a woman half her biological age.

"Lana, my darling Lana. You are wise beyond your years and this you have shown yet again. I could not find the voice to tell you what I feel and had you not shown the wisdom you have in suggesting we meet on this plain, I would not be telling you what I now must. After you all went to bed last night I took Monique to her room and tucked her in, as I would have done when she was a child. As she drifted into sleep she called out for them to leave Gwen alone. At first I was unsure of what she meant and I looked into her mind. She was unable to block my intrusion in her sleep, and I found within her memory a scene which had taken place on Le Selleur's ship." Ordinarily Mémé would have stopped there, her physical mind would have halted her spiritual one and she would have thought better of telling me. Part of me wished she would, but then I realised that I needed to know - she had news of my parents. "I saw a scene in which Monique physically blocked your parents from the gendarmes of The Sergeant, and then I heard a voice that I had never heard before yet knew instinctively. It was a cold cruel voice that resonated through every bone in my body. It was The Sergeant. He told Monique that he did not have the need to hurt them he was merely holding them; bait to trap us, all of us. He knows that you love them deeply and you will do anything to save them, and that out of our love for you we will help you. He has a new plan. He is trying to lure us into a trap." Her physical body slumped on the bench, I knew she could not keep the disconnection between physical and metaphysical much longer and I found my spirit drifting back towards my body. I let it happen, guiding her back to the ground as I went. Mémé needed guidance for once, and although the Matriarch is traditionally the strongest within the family, it was up to me to take charge for the time being. Once back on the earthly plain, I helped Mémé to her bedroom and went to my own to get dressed.

CHAPTER SEVEN

Christmas and Birthdays Come at Once

I hurriedly got dressed, I needed to think, to plan, to sort out the best thing to do. Mémé was in no fit state to take charge and she knew it. The act of me putting her to bed signalled a change over of power; well perhaps signal wasn't the right word. I felt the power pulsate through my body, charging my spirit in a way I had never thought possible. I may not have gained the knowledge of the Matriarch but I had gained the added experience of power, something that would be of help in the future. Admittedly I hadn't expected it and it was definitely something I would not have asked for. It was an exchange that however temporary the others would instantly recognise. For the time being, I had become the Matriarch. The power would ordinarily have scared me, but I had no time to be scared. I had things to figure out and I had to do them now. I searched through my bedroom for things I may need and pulled out the chest with my inherited tools inside. In doing so I knocked the family photo album from the shelf and before I could pick it up I saw something on the page which it had landed open at. It was the second page from the back, and upon its surface lay an image I had never seen before. It was a picture of a planet, no a star covered in life. I know, I know, stars are burning gaseous balls that by the time their light reaches the Earth have probably burnt out. But there it was. It couldn't have been a planet, it wasn't big enough, and there were no moons or suns within the vicinity, yet it seemed to have a gravitational pull and an endless light supply. I suddenly realised why I hated the dark - Laterrétoile was a place where the light always shone - there was no darkness. It looked beautiful. My ancestral home was the earthstar, a place where human life flourished and lived longer due to the eternal light. It explained why Mémé could

live so long and have children so late in life.
I hated knowing that it was under a Hitler-
type regime and I wanted it to be free. How
this information about the planet's light
supply was going to help me I wasn't sure.
But I knew that it was important.

I took the chest and the album into
the study and sat at the desk not sure what
to do next. I may have had the matriarchal
power but I was not sure how to use it. I
began by taking the items out of my trunk
and reached the polished stick that Mémé
had made for me. I knew now that it was in
fact a wand, a highly spiritual item used in
the casting of various spells and making of
various potions. It was also an item that was
made out of the purest form of positive
energy - love. I sat, twiddling it through my
fingers, the energy radiating from it was
immense, yet I felt connected, before I had
entered into the fold of the Magiques once
more I would have dropped it. Instead it
was calming to know that I could control
something so powerful and so important. I
stood up, walked over to the bookcase
behind the desk and gently ran the tip of the
wand along the books. I wasn't sure what I
should be expecting, but my persipacité

sixiéme told me that I was doing the right thing. I walked along the shelves for what seemed like an age, and then it happened. The tip of my wand reached a book, which suddenly glowed, showing a title that had not been perceptible to the human eye: 'L'histoire de la famille Cornique.' I wasn't sure what help it would be but I lifted it from the shelf and put it on the desk. But before I got to look at it I had a telepathic message from Kara, 'Lana, meet me in the first lounge.'

*

I raced down the corridors, I instinctively knew that there was a problem; I hadn't felt any thought waves towards Mémé. Perhaps she had already told the others. I couldn't be sure that she hadn't but I did not think she had. Perhaps the power exchange had created a ripple effect, which hit the others. It would explain why I felt Mémé's life force asleep in her room. The rhythmic breathing hadn't faltered since I had watched her fall into an instant sleep. When I got to the living room I found Kara sitting there, her face contorted into a look of anguish and concern. Monique was lying on one of the couches in a state of unconsciousness.

"Lana, I came in here and found her like that. I ... I tried to heal her but I couldn't. She won't wake. I've tried...I've tried." She was shaking with fear. Something wasn't right and she knew it. I walked over to Monique, knelt beside her and placed my hands on her chest. She was breathing and her heartbeat was regular. This wasn't a health problem, that's why Kara hadn't been able to help. The psychosis under the influence of which Monique was currently suffering was to all intents and purposes self-inflicted. How I knew that I wasn't sure but it was staring me in the face. Monique's mind had shut itself down in order to escape the horrors that she had seen in the past months. Her mind and body needed to recuperate from the torture she had received in the confines of the ship and consequently she had gone into a magically induced state of catatonia. There was nothing we could do for her except allow the coma to take its course. I told Kara to get a blanket and some cushions; I wasn't going to attempt to move my comatose aunt, even with my telekinetic powers. She was best left where she was, any sudden movement could have sent her body into shock, and even with the combined forces of mine and Kara's healing powers, I wasn't sure we would be able to save her. The next thing I did was to get Tim to bring my things in from the study. I was going to need to keep a close eye on Monique but continue my research efforts so that I could work out a plan that would bring back Mum and Dad without risking the capture of the entire family.

*

A couple of days later, I sat in the living room at some early hour of the morning, making an entry into my diary. There had been no improvement in Monique's condition and I was severely beginning to doubt my abilities as the temporary Matriarch. I decided to spend some quality time sorting out my thoughts and allowing my struggles to come out. I cannot possibly re-write the entry into plainer words so here you go:

It's now three in the morning, or thereabouts, I don't have my watch as the battery died yesterday and I'm not completely sure of the clock on the mantel at the moment. Monique still hasn't come round, I'm not sure if she ever will. I fear we may have lost her for good. I know I didn't believe her story completely at first, but now I see she had to be telling what she saw as the truth. She would not have fallen into a trance-like sleep. Her brain and body have had enough, and if she doesn't come round soon they may shut down forever. My newly acquired powers are draining to say the least and consequently I am getting tired quicker than usual. Having to cope with the added responsibility is not easy. I mean I am, but I am no longer responsible for just me - I have seven other people depending on me and that is the hardest thing of all to contend with. All I want is to do is fall asleep for a couple of weeks, but I need to continue my research. If it were ordinary homework I would have finished by now, but the fact I haven't yet found the answer is driving me mad! So far I haven't come up with anything that appears to be wholly relevant. I mean I can see how this history junk may be of benefit later but right now I need something I can use against The Sergeant! This is absolutely useless! I'm normally not a quitter, but I'm so close to jacking in the whole thing - I mean it's not like I had any choice in being who I am! I accept that my destiny will catch up with me wherever I am, but I wasn't expecting to become Matriarch as well! I'm only 14! Hang on a minute, am I still fourteen? What's the date?

At that point the diary entry stops cos I got up and ran into the kitchen to check the calendar. Was it January already? Where had time gone? We'd missed Christmas and Yule and I was going to be fifteen in like less than twenty hours! How could we have missed the New Year and the important family holiday season? Something had to be done about it. The family needed cheering up, I needed a break and maybe some sort of joint celebration would bring Monique round. My research was put on the back burner. I started planning a late Christmas/Yule and birthday party for the next day. Gone was my tired stupor of researching endlessly and I began to frantically organise things. I checked the food supplies in the kitchen and discovered that our cupboards were still over flowing with food and that there was a fridge and freezer in the pantry that were somehow running without electricity. I would keep the others out of the main lounge for the day and turn it into a grotto of good cheer. I moved the couch on which Monique lay to the side of the room as carefully as possible, stopping at intervals to make sure she wasn't suffering adverse effects from the repositioning. It was only four o'clock, I had time to go to the garden and bring through one of the fir trees it held. I ran through the corridors swiftly and silently. I pulled a pot out of the garden shed and managed to remove the medium sized tree from the ground and put it in the pot with telekinesis and then used the power to carry it back to the first living room. Then I went back up the corridor, into my room, quickly typed up a family memo and printed it off before sealing the lounge with a simple charm that I had picked up whilst teaching myself to control my powers. It was simple but unbreakable; the only one who would be able to get in and out of the room was me. They would only be able to get through after I had lifted it. Monique was trapped inside, but that wasn't a problem considering her current state.

I spent a sleepless twenty-eight hours preparing decorations, food and a generally festive scene. I made individual presents for all the family out of whatever was available, and if I do say so myself, they were the best presents I could possibly have gotten anyone. I made them each an individually different five-pointed star to represent Laterrétoile and a little something beside. An amulet for Maman to ward off feelings of self-doubt and guilt for giving me up, she was still having problems accepting that I had no bitter feelings towards her for doing what she had. A bead necklace for Kara, one that during the making of, I had cast a spell of protection. As much as I love my aunt she can be rather impulsive and the necklace was to help keep her safe. For Tim a set of runes using a third of the hematite from my precious gems collection, he is particularly talented with divination and his old runes had definitely seen better days. Monique's present was another amulet, this one was made to keep away the evil of bad dreams and enable her to find the peace of mind she so obviously needed. Mémé's gift was the hardest to make and took the longest to do. I took a plain wooden chalice from the

Magique supply cupboard, one I knew had never been used, and engraved it with the names of each of her children and put my name on the bottom. It was worth it because of the love I put into it as I chipped away the layer of wood and because I knew she would appreciate it more than any other gift I could have given her.

*

The others, as my memo asked, were waiting for me when I removed the charm from the door.

"Lana, what's going on? Why have you been locked up in there? Has something happened to Monique?" Mémé looked at me with an eye of concern. She may not be the working Matriarch, but she was obviously finding it hard to deal with the fact that she had relinquished her powers, even though she thought it was for the best.

"Nothing's wrong Mémé. I just realised that we had missed the festive season, and I decided that a late celebration was better than not having one at all." I kept the wanting to celebrate my birthday with my biological family for the first time ever a secret. After all if they had lost track of the date and forgotten then it wasn't fair of me to push it on them. They entered the living room and their jaws dropped in unison. I had transformed the room into an Aladdin's cave of Christmas and Yule. There wasn't an inch I hadn't decorated, and Mémé's was looking younger than she had in weeks. It was definitely the mood lifter they had needed.

We spent all day eating and laughing. There was no thought of The Sergeant and his army; it was just a big family party. As we sat down to a tea of ham and cucumber sandwiches and homemade mince pies with steaming mugs of hot chocolate, I handed out the presents. As Maman, Mémé, Kara and Tim opened theirs, I placed Monique's star under one of her hands and put the amulet around her neck. I had expected it to help her recovery, but the response was quicker than I ever thought it would be. Her eyes opened and she looked around.

"Thank you Lana. They're beautiful. But why are we getting presents on *your* birthday?" Mémé's jaw dropped for the second time that day.

"Your birthday! Oh Lana! How could I have forgotten your birthday? A Magique's fifteenth is one of the most important birthdays they will ever have, and I forgot it!" She was distraught.

"It's ok Mémé. Open your other present. I'm having the best possible birthday I could have. You're all happy and that makes me happy."

"But...but I ... I should have spent today with you. I should have been focusing my energy on you. You've become an adult in the world of Les Magiques and I ignored it!"

"Maman, she said she's having the best day she could ever have! You relinquished your matriarchal powers to Lana and she has chosen how to celebrate for the best. She has chosen and you should accept it." Maman spoke to Mémé gently and reassuringly. Mémé could see she was right and set about opening her Chalice. I had never known my grandmother to back down so quickly. I began to fuss over Monique, making sure she had food and drink. As make-do Matriarch it was my duty to do so and it felt natural to look after her. I only stopped when I heard Tim.

"Lana, they're beautiful. I needed a new set and they're perfect. My favourite stone, and the gold lettering." If I didn't know any better, by his reaction I would have said Tim was female. But my uncle is definitely one of the dreamers in life and his reaction was typical.

"You're welcome Tim. They were an inspired moment after seeing you use your old set. The flaky paint cannot help with the interpretations."

"Lana, the chalice is perfect. It's so carefully done. Thank you."

"The necklace, it's made out of my favourite colours!"

"This amulet is beautiful!"

"Look, the stars are all the same but subtly different!" This went on for a while. In fact it went on for about half an hour. By the time it finished, I was completely red in the face and ready for bed. I made my apologies and went off down the bedroom corridor to my room, where fully clothed I collapsed into a deep sleep.

*

It was about an hour later that I was

woken by Maman coming into my room. She quietly opened the door and tiptoed over to my bed. Had I not been woken by my heightened matriarchal senses I would have slept through until morning. Instead I sat up and looked her in the eye.

"Maman, what's wrong? Is everyone ok?"

"Everything's fine ma petite, I was just going to leave you this and let you sleep." She handed me a parcel wrapped in the most beautiful metallic purple paper I had ever seen. "I did not forget your birthday. I was going to give this to you this morning but you had worked so hard on making the day special for the rest of us I decided to wait." I unwrapped it carefully and gasped with surprise. Inside the paper were the most beautiful things I had ever seen. She had obviously spent hours in putting the gift together. There was a photograph album filled with pictures of my adoptive family, a framed photo of her holding me as a baby, a set of handmade silver jewellery - earrings, a necklace and bracelet, each adorned with the same style of interlocking star I had made for everyone, and perhaps the most special of all was her

Magique journal from when she had been my age. In it were the protection spells she had cast for me when she was carrying me and a list of all the names she had wanted to call me. As I looked at the beautiful name page, I found one circled - Lunegosse. I stared at her quizzically. My name was Lana and yet it did not appear on the page.

"It's your real name Lana. You are the moonchild. The foretold saviour and it seemed fitting. It is the name under which you were presented to La Mére Eternelle. We called you Lana as a nickname, one that would be more fitting within the outside world."

"It's beautiful, Maman. It's beautiful." The tears began welling up in my eyes and the strain of being Matriarch surfaced. I knew how Mémé must have felt when things got too tough. The difference was she had no one to turn to. I sat there and fell into my mother's arms and sobbed. The release of emotion was more powerful than ever before. Maman wrapped her arms around me and allowed me to weep. She did not question why, she merely sat there and accepted it. For the first time since Mémé had transferred her powers to me I was showing weakness. My mother was at that moment the protector not the protected and I became the child I had been before facing the added responsibilities that the Matriarch holds. For the first time in months, I was just me - Lunegosse.

CHAPTER EIGHT

Planning Begins

About a month later I lay in bed flipping through the pages of the birthday photo album and suddenly it hit me! How could I have been so blind? I couldn't believe I hadn't seen it before! I sent a thought wave out to Mémé and was practically shouting it with the force at which it left my brain. She came hurtling down to my room quicker than should have been possible for a woman of her age.

"Lana. What could be so...?"

"Can we get my brothers and sister down here? Is there a way of contacting Aunt Sophie? I think I may have it. Well part of it."

"Lana you're not making much sense."

"Perhaps not, but you'll see. And my name's not Lana so stop acting as if it is! My name's Lunegosse!"

"Sorry Lana, I mean Lunegosse. Why are you so insistent on using your full name all of a sudden?" She looked confused.

"I'm sorry Mémé. It's just that it feels right to use it. I mean Lana doesn't sound like the name of a prophesised child. It sounds like some normal fourteen year old who's sick of being called Alana. My name was given to me for a reason and whilst I may not be able to use it in the outside world I want to be able to down here. I did not mean to sound angry or defensive."

"It's alright my child. You want your brothers and sister here? I can do that I believe. Anything else you need?"

"Actually yes. Can you see if Catharine's mum will let her come for a couple of weeks? I know she'll miss school, but I can give her some tuition whilst she's down here. I'm gonna need her help with this one." Mémé frowned for a minute.

"I'll try, but I cannot guarantee that I can get her mother's approval as well." With that she left the room and I was left to sit and formulate the plan that was beginning to

come together in my head. It was another
night that I was sure I had fallen to sleep
well after the sun had risen in the outside
world.

*

      I awoke after a few hours of shallow
sleep and went to the kitchen to get a hot
cup of regular tea. I was in desperate need
of a pick-me-up that contained caffeine. The
fact that I rarely slept for longer than four
hours at a time and then was up for at least
twenty-four in between meant that I was
heavily dependant on that first cuppa of the
day. Sleep had become less of a necessity
than being awake and it was beginning to
show physically. I had my first grey hairs
streaking the blond. You may laugh, but
even though I was just fifteen, I had more
weight on my shoulders than I hope you
ever have to deal with. I got to the lounge to
discover that there was a fresh pot of caffeine
on the go and that Mémé had managed to
bring James and John, Sam and Catharine to
La Grotte. I slumped into the nearest chair
to the teapot and poured myself an extra
large serving before speaking. My adoptive

siblings and Catharine waited patiently, they all knew that I couldn't function without it. I asked Mémé if she would leave us, I knew I would have to explain later, but she did not need to know every detail of my plan, in fact it was best if she did not. I needed to protect her and the other Magiques from as much as possible. She obliged without question.

Before I got down to the serious business I had to discuss with them, I got up from my chair and hugged each of them in turn. It was so good to be in the same room as the people I had known and loved my entire life. I revelled in the fact that I could hold them and feel their life forces so close to my own. It took me a while to come down off of cloud nine and talk about why I needed them there.

"Guys, I know you're all wondering why you're here, and half the stuff I'm about to tell you will sound so strange you won't believe it, but I promise you it's true. I have never lied to any of you and never would. Catharine, before I start I want to apologise for keeping you in the dark until now. You have always been there for me and it hurts that I had to keep it from you but I know you will understand why I had to once I've explained."

"Lana, I would never hold anything against you. You did what you thought best and I accept that. You better not tutor me like Mrs H promised Mum though, or there'll be hell to pay! Why did you pull us all down here?" They sat in rapture as I told them everything that I have told you since beginning this letter. They made a good audience, none of them questioning what I was saying, but reacting at the appropriate places. When I had finished Sam looked at me, her green eyes pensive.

"Lana, my darling sister. I knew much of what you had just said when you came to us. Mum and Dad couldn't keep it from me. The years between you and I made them realise that I may have a problem with another sibling. They wanted to include me as much as possible. I was three when you turned up and already fed up with the twins, so they dumbed it down for me, filling in the blanks as I got older. I admit that they themselves did not know all that you have told us, but they thought they were doing what was best I expect. It meant that I could keep an extra eye on you for them." She looked as if she'd said too much and was regretting it. I told her not to worry I did not hold anything against her - she was right - they had done what they thought best, and I now had to do the same for them and my biological family.

"I need your help in pulling off the greatest scheme we will ever have worked on. Yes James, greater than the Halloween sweet heist of 1990 - although it was a brilliant plan. This time Mum and Dad are depending on us with their very lives in the balance, and the lives of my biological family. We get Mum and Dad back, and I can concentrate on the task I was prophesised to complete. We need to act fast."

"Ok, what do you want us to do?" John looked highly thrilled at the prospect of pulling off a new scheme. What he and (James by the looks of things) had failed to realise was that this one was going to be dangerous.

"Listen carefully as I don't have it fully formulated yet and that's one of the places where you come in. As usual I need you two for the diversion part of the plan." I looked at the twins. "You are experts in this field and I haven't got the diversion scripted as I'm sure you can manage it on your own steam."

"Why thank you oh prophesised one!" I hadn't seen the two of them do the double speak thing for a while, and they bowed the same cheeky bow. I realised in that moment just how much I had missed them. They seemed almost caricatures of the way I remembered them. Almost as if they had been taken out of a child's book.

"Catharine do you remember the science lesson when we discussed the probability of cloaking devices?" She nodded. "I need you to search your science book for the notes we took, take a look at the weaknesses of such a device and let me know what you think. I may have a fairly good knowledge of things, but science is your specialty. Sam, do you remember the water balloon fights we had as kids? I need you to work on some sort of projectile device. Something more advanced than the catapult and canon we used. I need something designed that will pack a wallop." Each of them took their responsibilities with an air of gravity that showed how much they wanted to help. Even the twins with their slapstick comedy were more serious than I had ever seen them. Today was the day that all of us became more than just siblings and childhood friends. Today we united in a struggle bigger than any we had ever faced. It was in that instant I saw the others in a new light. They became what I had already become - adults within their own right.

*

As my friend and adoptive family worked on their individual task, I resumed my research, this time with help from my mother, aunts and uncle. We spent hours pouring over the Magique journals in the library in hopes of finding potions and spells. Anything that would help us locate Mum and Dad. Mémé supplied both groups with constant nourishment, taking a step back and allowing me a free reign over what was happening. She was not happy in doing so, but I would need her help at a later, much more important stage and I needed her to be at her best when the time came. I insisted that everyone take regular breaks apart from myself. If I got any sleep, it was a quick catnap here and there. I was always the first one up and the last one to bed when

I went to bed, and then after two or three hours I was up again. It got to the point where I was running on caffeine, chocolate and adrenaline and not much more. In fact the twins made me a sign for my door during one of their breaks, which read; *'There's too much blood in my caffeine system.* It brought some much needed laughter into the otherwise work-filled atmosphere under which we were all living.

No one but me had a full picture of the plan that was coming to fruition as we toiled endlessly, but that was, as I wanted it. If everyone knew everything, it would pose as a weakness when things came to a head and we went into action. As well as the research I was doing I was also screening the work the others were doing. Every night, Catharine gave me a new list of possible weaknesses, Sam presented me with a new weapon of assault diagram, the twins would give me a written diversion plan and I'd receive a list of possible spells and potions from Les Magiques. It took me hours to assess the possibility of each in turn and often I found flaws that meant it wasn't possible for us to use whatever they had come up with. If it was usable in any form then it was placed on a maybe pile because it was possible that a bit of one thing and a part from another would work in conjunction. After a month of research I sat one night looking at the maybe pile. I say night but it was in fact early morning, it was just that I hadn't seen my bed in about thirty hours and it hadn't quite hit sunrise outside. I was sat in the subterranean garden, which was lit by small torches poking out from the ground with what must have been my fortieth helping of caffeine since I had woken up the last time. I had a notebook on my lap, a pen in one hand and a piece of paper in the other. If I was to take the first line of the spell on the page I was holding and then pair it off with the second line of the one which was sitting on top of the pile on the bench then maybe I could add the third line from the one I had just placed aside and have the start of a more powerful deflection spell. Sounds confusing to you? I was in a state of manic concentration and wasn't sure if I was making sense myself. All I knew for certain was that sleep had to wait until I had gone through the pile and looking at its thickness, I would be there for at least another four hours. The bottles of coke sitting at my feet would help me keep going, of that I was sure, and then it would another catnap before continuing the endless search for weapons in the upcoming battle.

*

I did not last until the end of the pile however. Mémé came into the garden at about eight o'clock carrying a blanket and a pillow. She must have moved the piles onto the ground and lain me down because when I came round it was three in the afternoon and I was feeling more rested than I had in ages. I had a major caffeine hangover, but other than that I was thinking clearer than had been possible previously and was able to finish the pile with ease. Writing the rest of the deflection spell and making suggested improvements and combinations for the weapon. By the time I finished it was about seven-thirty and I made my way down to the primary living room calling Les Magiques by thought and asking them to get the others on the way. We were going to have a proper meal together for the first time since my birthday. We needed to have an evening off to lighten the stress on us all and just to give us time to relax. It was a time for me to find out how things were going in the outside world, to let my hair down and for a moment forget that sooner or later we would all be facing the terror of The Sergeant in an unavoidable way. For those precious two hours when we sat laughing and eating, I became Lana again. I wasn't Lunegosse, saviour of Laterrétoile; I was Lana, sister, daughter, granddaughter and friend. I sat revelling in the fact that so many loved ones surrounded me. Monique was looking better. She had a healthy glow in her cheeks and was smiling constantly as Sam and the boys recounted childhood tales of what I had been like as a little girl. Maman's attitude was lighter than it had been in the months since I had met her. She was cheerful and the doubts she had held previously seemed to have vanished. Tim was acting the clown - showing the boys sleight of hand tricks and telling them the best way to launch a water bomb attack - if Mum could have heard him she would have been shooting daggers from her eyes. Mum... Mum and Dad were still stuck somewhere in space under the hand of Le Selleur. I wished they were not. Dad would have enjoyed the scene of frivolity and carefree people laughing together. My happiness ended in that moment. As the thought hit me I became consumed by the nagging that had been attacking ever since I had become Matriarch. How could I save my parents and keep the others safe? I needed to hit the books again. To find a plan that wouldn't fail. I made my excuses and left. I couldn't sit idly by and allow things to escape me.

The need in my heart to get to my parents was overwhelming when combined with the desperate wish to make sure everyone I loved was safe. How could I penetrate that shield? I grabbed Catharine's notes from the desk in the study, and the Magique journal containing the penetration spells and went back to the garden where my four two-litre bottles of coke sat untouched. If it took all night then I would come up with a start for the plan. I would *not* allow Mum and Dad to spend a moment longer than necessary in captivity, even if it meant that I did not sleep until I found them and brought them back to the safety of La Grotte. They were going to come back safe and sound, of that I was sure the question was how?

*

The study lark was hard going, several times I thought I had the right answer, only to find on closer inspection that there was an obvious insurmountable problem that would make us easy targets for the opposition. I drew diagrams of various attacks that looked like possibilities and earmarked various potions and spells that when aimed at the weak spots identified by Catharine would hopefully cause the magical shield of the ship to falter and die, enabling me to get on board. I had decided that I was not going to allow anyone else on the ship - it was far too dangerous, and it was more likely that I would be able to get out of a sticky situation than any of the others, even with the powers my biological family possessed. I have always been small and agile and it would be easy for me to escape from any hold they got on me, especially with my combined powers. The others may not be so lucky. They would be able to help me penetrate the ships defences from the ground. After going through all the potions and spells that I had earmarked, I chose three of each that showed the most promise. Yet I knew instinctively that I would as they stood at the moment they would not be anywhere near strong enough individually. I now had to go to the small room off of the study and work on combining elements of the potions and seeing if they would react in the correct way. It was the toughest thing I had done so far in the planning stages. The necessity of proving a combined potion's capability meant that I had to try it on various difficulties of magical deflection shield. Starting with the simplest form that could be easily broken, if it did not break that then there was something majorly wrong with the potion and it meant that I had to start all over again. The stress levels within me were rising with each failed potion and I was beginning to feel the strain more than ever before. Every time I thought I had cracked it because the potion that I was currently using had outstripped the others it failed to pass the next level of the testing. I spent six hours without a break searching for the right formula and my eyes were beginning to itch because of the energy I was putting into he development of the perfect potion. It wasn't until I realised that I was desperate for the toilet that I allowed myself to take a break. The break which I intended to last only long enough for me to get to the bathroom and back but I got stopped on the way back from the bathroom by Mémé.

"Lunegosse my darling, are you still at it? Come and have some food. You need to eat."

"I don't have time, I have to work this out now. The plan is coming together slower than I would like and I need to get this part finished today."

"Lunegosse Mathilde Cornique Le Monnier! I know you are taking your matriarchal responsibilities seriously but you need to eat. I am talking as your grandmother not as one of the people you are currently responsible for. If you do not eat something substantial you will collapse from exhaustion and what use will you be to anyone then?" She peered over the top of her reading glasses at me with a stare, which said 'defy me and you won't like what you see'. I gave in and followed her through to the first lounge. I may be in charge of the lives of eleven people but she still had the grandmother prerogative and that meant that once in a while I had to do as she said. And anyway she was right, I needed to eat something, the remaining two bottles of coke I had left would not keep me going for long. Mémé disappeared into the kitchen and came back five minutes later with a bowl of steaming hot leek and potato and soup, some slices of baguette and a glass of freshly squeezed orange juice which had come from the oranges growing in the garden. I sat down and ate for all my life was worth. The meal vanished just as quickly as it had been brought out, regardless of the temperature of the soup. It was nice to eat something that warmed me to the bone and would keep me going for longer than the caffeine and sugar of the coke that had so far kept me running in conjunction with my determination and the adrenaline running through my veins. I made to get up and go back to the supply room as soon as I had finished, but Mémé fixed me once more with her impenetrable stare and I slumped back into the armchair. I wasn't going to argue, my senses, even without their higher state of awareness would have been able to pick up the 'take charge' waves vibrating from my grandmother's eyes.

"Lana, yes I said Lana, you are going to sit here and take a break for a while. I will continue with the potion trials and you can take a couple of hours off. I am not saying sleep, as I am sure that would be impossible with the amount of caffeine you have pumped your body with today. Read a magazine or a book, do some schoolwork, just take a break before you run yourself completely into the ground. The power that I gave you were those which unlocked the ones you would not have discovered for a considerable time if your development had been allowed to take its natural course. You were born to become Matriarch as well as our people's saviour, and the two lots of responsibilities are beginning to take their toll. No fifteen year old should have grey hair and wrinkles, and you my darling petite-fille have both. I know that it is part and parcel of who you are and who you must become, but if you don't take regular breaks from the task at hand then you will beat me to la tombe. And I don't want to have to bury my own grandchild." Her words were those of concern and I couldn't argue with her. My mind was tired and emotionally I was stretched as far as my nerves would allow. I let her take on my task at hand and went to my room to get my laptop and a DVD to watch. Just like the fridge and freezer that were running without electricity, my laptop's battery was constantly charged and hadn't died since I had entered La Grotte.

*

I must have fallen asleep after a couple of hours watching DVDs, because the next thing I knew, Mémé came in looking distinctly dishevelled and collapsed next to me, almost sending the laptop flying. I knew instantly that she had cracked it. There was a tired look of accomplishment in her eyes and even though I knew she was just about ready to call it a day, I insisted on seeing it work. She took me back to the potions store and performed the most complicated of defence charms. Then she picked up a vial of a sludgy green mixture and saying a few words from one of the penetration spells through the vile at the shield. Nothing happened for a second and then the shield begin to fizz and crackle, within a minute it had disappeared and was not returning. Finally part of the plan was in place. Now I had to speak to Sam about the projectile weapon that we would fire the potion from. It needed to be small and compact and easy to use, but powerful at the same time. I would start working on finding the ship the next day. My body was still tired and needed rejuvenating before I faced another onslaught of pieces and pieces of paper with different scrying techniques on them. I would be glad when things were sorted and we could get Mum and Dad back with us.

CHAPTER NINE

The Flaw in the Plan

I slept for a full twelve hours that night; I couldn't believe how tired I had actually been. It's true that studying can really take it out of you and up until the following morning I wouldn't have believed. I knew that I had been working constantly with hardly any relaxation time, but I had been taking things in my stride as far as possible, even with the strain I had been feeling I had not wanted to admit to myself just how difficult things were. I was used to being able to finish things quickly and easily and admitting to myself that I was finding things hard had not been simple as my old school work. The realisation hit like a ten-ton freight train smashing into a brick wall. It wasn't the nicest of feelings that's for sure. I had the worst headache imaginable - I swore there and then to limit the amount of caffeine that I allowed to enter my body. If this was going to be the aftermath I was not going to rely so heavily on coke and coffee to get me through the day. From now on I was going to drink herbal tea, hot chocolate and the *occasional* cup of caffeine. Right now I needed breakfast, something healthy - like I'd eat anything else! I hadn't done any dance related work for a while and consequently the extra sugar I'd been consuming was definitely taking its toll on my body. I made my way to the kitchen, poured myself an extra large orange juice - good for rehydration and had a small breakfast of a banana and a couple of apples. I needed the carbs and would eat a fuller meal at lunch. Right now I needed to exercise. The only cure I've ever known for over indulgence is abstinence and I hadn't kept away from the foods, I should have known better. Don't get me wrong, I think all foods are good for you in moderation - I know I sound like some tyrannical adult whinging at you for eating too many sweets, but I'm only five feet one tall and generally small boned so I had managed to put on more weight than normal, even though stress usually causes you to lose weight. Now listen to me, I sound like I'm advocating starving yourself. It's not that either. You have to take care of your body, and then it will take care of you.

I grabbed the stereo from the kitchen table and walked into the living room. Admittedly I was still tired; otherwise I would have cleared some space the traditional way. Instead I used my telekinesis to clear a large enough space for me to work out in. It was about half eight, the others were still in bed - we had all been working long hours trying to sort out the plan. They could sleep for a while longer; I preferred not to be interrupted anyway. I know I'm a dancer, but the sight of me in a leotard and dance tights is not something I'd wish on my worst enemy (well maybe The Sergeant!). My work out was simple enough, some stretches, a few basic dance moves - nothing too strenuous as my body couldn't handle it. But soon I was feeling much better and more alert and ready for action than I had in days. Time for a quick shower and then back to work.

*

Sam came into the study at about ten o'clock with a list of the various ideas she had had. There were diagrams to back them up. The problem was that they were all far too large and therefore easily detectable. We together for three hours trying to find a way to shrink down the existing scales and use one of the weapons she had designed. The problem was that the smaller they got, the less power they held which meant that I would have to use a potion or spell to charm the weapon and that in itself would cause problems. If the weapon was magically charged and the potion vial it contained leaked then the two energies could combine and the whole thing would become highly unpredictable unless enough research into which charm to use was done. I could have put Maman and the others on to it, but we were running out of time. I had to call everyone into the study; we were all going to have to work on this part of the plan. I knew we'd find an answer it just needed everyone's full attention.

"What's up Lunegosse? How come you needed us all here?" Tim burst into the room, followed by the twins, Maman, Monique, Mémé, Catharine and Kara.

"I didn't... oh wait!" How thick was I being? Matriarchal powers - if I thought I needed something easily accessible (including people), it would show. "I need all hands on deck," James and John put their hands on the floor. "Not that sort of deck. Honestly! Will you two ever grow up? I need everyone focused on the projectile weapon. It needs to be compact but powerful. Monique, Mémé, Maman, and Catharine I want you to research shrinking charms. Anything that might enable us to use one of the existing plans." They took the plans off of Sam and set to work. "Boys, yes that includes you Tim. I want you to work with Sam and Kara on new plans. Remember it has to be small."

"What about you? What are you going to work on?" Kara asked gently.

"I'm going to work on the finer details of the plan. You know, what happens when I've actually got aboard Le Selleur's ship. But first, I'm going to go and get lunch for everyone and bring it back through here so we can eat and work at the same time. No I am not making double quarter pounder cheeseburgers for you two. You'll have what everyone else is having. Any arguments and when Mum gets back, I'll tell her where you keep your magazines. And I'm not talking about the wrestling ones!" I left them to get started. James and John were sitting nonplussed, trying to work out how I knew about their secret stash. In truth I had found out when they first came to La Grotte. The different frequency of non-famial thought waves had pulsated through my body, and John had been pining for his usual fix of what he thought was magazine heaven. He had been wondering if there would be a male relative of mine who would have such a stash living with us. Tim however, is more interested in magic and literature and more conservative forms of entertainment.

*

I returned to the study with three trays laden down with herbal teas, plates of salad, yoghurts and cutlery. The twins's faces dropped at the sight of the healthy meal, but Mémé gave them a sharp look and they tucked in without further complaint. I tucked myself away in the corner with a notebook and pen. I needed to concentrate on the finer points. Then I hit the biggest flaw imaginable. I should have realised sooner! I couldn't believe how I could have neglected what would be the biggest problem ever! I could prepare for the preliminary attack, but I knew nothing of the inside of the ship. I was going to have to ask Monique. And I knew within an instant that if I asked, she'd want to come with me and help me save my parents - she'd been feeling so guilty. But I couldn't put her in that danger! Oh what was I going to do? I sat clutching the notebook, peering over its edges, looking at the scene before me. The two mini task forces were hard at work, if I called Monique over, even by thought it would be too obvious. I couldn't believe that I had trapped myself in a corner. I lost the calm composure I had managed to gain whilst sorting people into groups and now that I found myself with a problem I freaked. Outwardly I must have looked ok because otherwise Mémé would have picked up on it. It was now that I felt the true strain of being Matriarch. Before now it had been not an easy ride but definitely easier to cope with. Under the pretence of going to the toilet and washing up the lunch things, I stacked up the washing up and trays and took them through to the kitchen. It was whilst standing at the sink that I burst into a flood of tears. With my eyesight blurred due to the weeping I let a plate slip from my hand it hit the granite floor with a smash. More mess to clear up. It set me into further floods, mixing the washing up water and the broken china with salty droplets. I picked up the broken glass with my powers; just to be sure I did not cut myself and that I got all of the pieces and then dropped it into the glass-recycling bin in the kitchen.

*

"Lunegosse, ça va? You have been gone so long I was starting to worry."

"Maman, you startled me! Ça va bien, merci beaucoup. I'm just tired. There's so much to do and not enough time to do it in." I forced a smile. I couldn't tell her my problem. I had to protect her, to protect all of them.

"Lunegosse, do you think I'm stupid? There's something that's bothering you. Don't look so surprised. I haven't entered

your head; you would have felt my presence.
It's my l'intuition maternelle telling me
something's wrong. Mothers know these
things ma petite. Why don't you stop
washing up and come and sit down at the
table?" I did as I was asked. Anything for a
quiet life.

"Maman, I'm fine. I already told you
that it's just the strain of the whole affair.
That's all, I swear."

"Lunegosse, Lana. You're not 'fine', I
know that just as well as you do. I promise
that I'm not going to have a go at you. I'm
not going to shout. I just what to know what
the problem is, I may be able to help." I
looked at her, those intense brown eyes
showing concern. Unlike Mémé's would
have done, Maman's eyes did not stare into
my soul. Not as fervently anyway.

"Maman, I can't. It's not that I don't
want to, but I can't risk endangering your
life, or the lives of anyone within these caves,
or those of my adoptive parents. I trust you,
I do, it's just that, well, I will be responsible if
anything goes wrong. I am not about to put
you into a situation you may not be able to
get out of. I'm not doing that to you or
Monique." I'd let it slip! I couldn't believe

that I had let my aunt's name slip!

"Monique…me and Monique. Lana, you need her help don't you? You don't know how to navigate your way around the ship without her. And you know that I won't let you go up on your own. Oh Lana! Why didn't you say anything?"

"That's precisely why I did not say anything, I was right. If I would have told you that I was planning to go up there alone, you and Mémé wouldn't have let me. You would have tried to stop me. And as for Monique, there is *no* way I am letting her come up with me - if they found out that she is not the clone, they'd kill her, and I'm not going to let that happen!" Tears began to leak out of the corner of my eye once more.

"Ma chéri, you are the Matriarch, we cannot go against your decisions, but we can advise you. Let me call Maman and Monique, maybe we can sit down and work something out. You may be in charge, but you are still my daughter, and you need help in sorting this out." Before I had a chance to argue, she had sent out a message to them both.

"Maman, you are definitely Mémé's daughter." I half-smiled as the words passed my lips. They were so much alike at times that I often wondered if they were mother and daughter or two halves of the same person.

*

The others arrived fairly quickly, and soon we were all sitting around the table drinking fresh mugs of peppermint tea, discussing the situation at hand. In all honesty, the conversation made me rather angry with myself. I had slipped up earlier whilst telling Maman that I was ok, and as Matriarch, I felt that I should have worked out the flaw in my plan sooner, I also considered myself to be severely at fault as I was sure I had failed in my duties. I sat listening to the conversation, not having much input because I was wrestling with my conscious and my earthly emotions were weighing me down. I was half tempted to astral, but whilst that would have freed my mind, when I returned to my body, I would, inevitably have to deal with the emotions that arose during the astral conversation and that would sap me of more energy than if I kept my metaphysical and physical selves together.

"Lunegosse, what do you think?"

"Huh? What?" I should have been concentrating - another failure on my part.

"Why doesn't Monique run over the layout of the ship with you and then you can go up alone?" Mémé asked, her blue eyes showing more love and respect than I ever thought possible.

"Sounds good…oh no, wait! She's going to have to come with me! Le Selleur's expecting the clone Monique to track me down. If Monique doesn't show, then he'll know that they switched! Oh Mére Eternelle! What are we going to do? I can't let Monique go up there, and I can't go up there alone! This is turning into the biggest fiasco ever! Everything seemed so simple before. Mémé you're going to have to take back the Matriarchal powers - I am not ready - I cannot do this!" I burst into floods again; the situation was really taking its toll on me.

"Lunegosse Mathilde! You are ready for this. The lack of self-confidence you are feeling is natural. It is not possible for anyone to foresee everything, even someone with the combined powers of saviour and Matriarch. So Monique has to go with you?

We'll give them Monique - just not the real one." Maman's face blanched, I picked up on her thoughts without even trying to. They were the same as mine - what if Le Selleur noticed?

"Don't worry, I'm not about to send anyone up there without Lunegosse's agreement. Just hear me out. If Mathilde takes Monique's place then she can do exactly what Monique did to get out. If she astrals she'll be fine. We send Monique up there and she'll be more susceptible to The Sergeant and his men. She has already been put through their torture methods once, and whilst she is recovering well, she would not stand up to it again just yet. Mathilde my darling, you are strong and fit. You are your sister's exact double, and as long as you are careful, you will be able to get to Jack and Gwen and back to Lunegosse before they figure out that something's wrong and before they manage to extract information from Lunegosse. We need to fine tune the plan, but I think, no I am sure that it is our only viable option and it *will* work." My grandmother had finally lost the plot! They were not going to extract information from me either! They were going to kill me at the first opportunity they got! I saw before me a raving lunatic. First she wanted to send me and my mother up onto a ship that was swarming with the enemy, and then she wanted us to separate on the ship! How were we going to pull this off and get off the ship without being detected? Admittedly I hadn't worked out how I was going to get myself and Mum and Dad off the ship, but to get Maman off as well - this was going to be a nightmare!

*

All my energies were now focused on memorising the layout of the ship. Maman was doing the same except her energies were divided into that and astral practice. The others still worked diligently on the tasks I had set them prior to my realisation that things were not working out the way that they should be. My head was in a spin. My brain so bogged down by the blueprints that lay within Monique's mind. What she knew of the ship wasn't as much as I would've hoped. However, it was all I had to go on and I would have to be extra vigilant whilst on board. If Maman was going to find my parents, then I had to master controlling her body via telekinesis, the only problem being that if I were discovered to be controlling her body then we would be caught. And so far in order to move anything when I wasn't angry I had to use my hands. I was having to push myself further than ever to gain control of the connection between the power and my mind. That and the fact I couldn't get the blueprints out of my head. It took about three weeks for me to get it, and during that time a lot had happened. Catharine had gone home, returning only on weekends - she couldn't afford to stay off school, and her mum wasn't happy about her being away so often. Tim had been suffering with a cold and was unable to put as much effort in as he wanted. I had overheard an argument he had had with Mémé one night as I made my way to bed. She was insisting that he rest for a while and take things easy, and he was insisting that he needed to be working. I actually agreed with Mémé, he was of no use to us if he was ill. Luckily I didn't need to get involved as Mémé won the argument and Tim was confined to his bedroom until he wasn't talking with a blocked nose and coughing up phlegm sporadically. Even the twins were suffering under the strain. Well perhaps suffering isn't the right word; they had definitely changed that was for sure. The usual cacophony of banter that they aimed at each other and the rest of us had ceased to be. Instead they kept their heads down and spent most of their time working way into the night. They had even stopped moaning about the healthy meals they were being supplied with. Mum would have fainted with shock at the amount of vegetables James and John were willing putting away. Dad was right, I was a good influence on them; just not in the way he had meant me to be.

*

It was mid-April when the plan finally came together. The weapon had been finished. It was compact and powerful without the need for magical shrinkage or a magic power boost. We had potions to stop the shield from working, disarm the weaponry and cause gaseous escape clouds. Spells to create illusions, render the opposition powerless and to take their powers away. I had even managed to master the power to freeze whole groups of people and to do it to everyone but those who were on my side. The ship had been located through the most complex of divinatory methods. Tim had used his scrying crystal, runes, tarot deck and the flame of a candle to create an extra powerful locating spell, one that I did not care to understand at present, he could explain once we had got my parents back. We were as ready as we ever would be. At least I hoped we were. There was nothing else we could do except for pray that we had everything covered. And since the workload had reduced to practically nothing in comparison to the amount of study and research everyone had put into the plan, I decided that we all deserved the evening off. We sat in the first living room and kicked back. Although it was not a celebration as such, there was an air of excitement, anticipation and triumph in the air. All we had to do now was to put the plan into action. That was the thing that turned my stomach as Tim sat playing the guitar and everyone joined in by singing along to the songs that changed alternately between modern music and the music of the sixties and seventies. Tomorrow would be the biggest day in all of our lives so far. For tomorrow was the day that we were to execute the plan and find out once and for all if we had worked out all the possible flaws. As Tim played his last song of the night, I sat staring into the flames of the fire I was sitting next to, my mind focusing on the moment when I would see my parents again.

CHAPTER TEN

The First of Many

As the sun rose in the spring sky I took my first steps into natural sunlight in months. The scenery around me had changed so much since I had entered La Grotte. The trees were sprouting leaves and blossom, the grass underneath my feet was lush and green once more, no longer frost bitten. In the neighbouring surroundings I heard the calls of young birds, begging their mothers to bring them food. It was breathtaking. Had I been able to stay where I was I would have liked to just stand and watch the scene lit with the first orange rays of the life giving sun. Instead I hurried to the edge of the clearing where the dolmen hiding our home stood and lingered there, waiting for Maman to arrive. The morning sun was warming and I was grateful of its powerful heat. The night's chill still hung in the air at the edge of the clearing and anything that removed the cold was welcome. I watched as Maman crept from the entrance to La Grotte and made her way towards me, dressed in one of Monique's dresses. It was bizarre, for the first time in a long while I realised once more how much alike my aunt and mother looked. She arrived within seconds of leaving the entrance and was quickly followed by the twins. At this moment her spirit soared above her body and she took control of her physical self from the astral plan. We made our way due south for about half an hour, the twins acting as lookouts, one scouting around in front and one behind. Both were wearing amulets charged to protect them from the evil magic of The Sergeant's forces. It was weird walking alongside Maman's body. It was moving but she was above us, it freaked me out a bit. But then it had to be done.

As we approached the field over which the ship was centred, the boys backed off into the trees, the distraction they were to create would occur later. Each of their amulets contained one of the hairs from my head and they would feel the amulet grow heavier when the time came for the diversion. I had to calm my heartbeat as we waited to be found. Any sign that we were planning something could ruin everything. I stood as if under a mobility spell, one that would have stopped my mind from controlling my body. We did not have long to wait. I felt my feet being lifted by an unseen force and was aware that it trapped Maman's spirit as well as her body. It would take all the self-control she could muster to stop the two from becoming joined as one again. Within moments we were standing in front of the most hideous man I had ever seen. Not a physical man, but not a ghost either. I was face to face with The Sergeant and in actuality he was rather diminutive in stature yet his face was enough reason for my heart to sink into my stomach. Two small beady black eyes that were *not* normal. They lacked the whites around the iris and where they should have been, instead the blackness continued. His nose was nothing more than two slits where the nostrils were meant to be. There was no protruding formation leading up to them. His mouth was lipless, just a gapping hole with no teeth. Had it not been for the fact that I was on a mission of the most importance I would have cowered.

"Well done my pet. You have completed your task and brought me a most excellent prize. Fetch me the one from who you were cloned and the couple who have raised this supposed saviour and you shall have your reward." His voice could have drawn blood from a stone. It was deep and rasping, it sound like metal scraping against metal. Maman obeyed and left the room. Ok so this was not how we had planned things but it might just make it easier for us to complete our task.

"I cannot believe that they thought a child would defeat me. You are nothing but a little girl." He ran an extremely knarled finger along by jaw line, it didn't quite touch me; instead I felt an icy cold wind brush against my face. "How can someone who has been so easily captured be the supposed saviour of an entire race? You have no power at all. You trusted your heart and followed a mere likeness of your aunt to this place. You cannot be that clever. How does it feel to meet the one person who can destroy you with the blink of an eyelid?" I said nothing. I simply stood, not blinking. He was not going to force me into an angry outburst. I wasn't stupid enough to allow my temper to rise as that could endanger the whole mission.

"Your silence shows that you are weak granddaughter of Lahela." Who? I was pretty sure I had never heard that name before. Let me see, Rachel, my adoptive grandmothers were called Doris and Edith, so no Lahelas in my families! "You have no real power that is obvious, and if you do it is lessened by your emotions. A human weakness, one that will reduce you to nothing eventually. You humans are so often controlled by your hearts instead of your minds, especially the females of your breed. You pose no threat to the smallest of insects, let alone a great ruler like me." Great ruler my backside!

"Emotions are a necessity in understanding yourself and those around you. Lack of emotional involvement is often the more dangerous position to be in." I did not blink but merely stood there. The Sergeant stood for a moment, unsure of the next move he should make. His logical mind could not understand the calmness of my voice as I had spoken. If he was expecting anything it was not that.

"Are you so sure of that enfant? It is your emotions that brought you here. The ridiculous notion that you can save the people who have raised you. You cannot save them, your taunte vrai or yourself. You have no means of escape. You are mine." His face contorted into what could only be described as a form of smile.

"Believe what you will. So far in my life, my emotions have taught me well. They tell me now that you cannot sustain your present form for much longer and that you will have to leave me to your chief of police. A Caporal Le Selleur I believe. He is human yet you trust him to carry out your work. If I am not mistaken there is the first flaw in your logic."

"You may think so, but Le Selleur is less human than you. He has undergone many hours of training to suppress his emotions. The only one he now possesses is that of anger. He has been drained of everything else. It serves my purposes that he retain the ability to raise his temper as it means that he can perform the punishments required for traitors and prisoners to undergo. It gives him a passion for his work."

"But is passion not another emotion? It is a separate entity from anger and whilst the two may occasionally combine, they cannot be described as the same thing. Again I find flaw with your logic. You claim to be a great ruler and I do not deny that you show many of the qualities of such a man, yet your logic is more fallible than you think it to be. A great ruler would be aware of his own faults as well as those of the beings around him." My temper was not rising as I spoke, however, his was. I knew that if I kept finding problems he would struggle to keep himself within the realm of the physical and if I managed it in time, he would not be able to call Le Selleur. His particular form of astral projection was hard to maintain and in order to recuperate he would have to remain silent for a fairly long period of time.

(Hang on! My brain suddenly caught hold of the whole Lahela thing! Of course Rachel couldn't be Mémé's real name, she would have to have had a pseudonym in the outside world so that she couldn't be detected as easily! I felt completely thick!)

"Trying to make me leave are you? Don't want me to call Le Selleur do you? Well I hate to disappoint you ma précieuse, but I have already called him and he is on his way. I am not as clueless as you would like to believe I am. He will be here after escorting the clone and her captives to me. I will not allow her to be duped by your aunt, that would create problems for me." Thank La Mére Eternelle! He hadn't twigged! He still believed Maman to be the clone. That was one less thing to worry about for the moment at least.

*

Moments later in walked Le Selleur, Maman, Mum, Dad and the clone. The tears welled up in Mum's eyes when she saw me. My heart raced at seeing her and Dad again, but I couldn't afford to show it outwardly - The Sergeant would play on it and I could guarantee that that would not be good. I wondered how things were going on the ground. Now that everything up here was falling into place it was essential that everyone on the ground was ready. The whole time I had been standing there, I had

had the weapon concealed in my hand. It was ridiculously small and I had had to keep a tight hold on it, as I was afraid of dropping it. My constant clenching of my right fist had been carefully mimicked by my left, with the hope of showing frustration and anger at the situation. This should enable me to keep the weapon concealed and to whip it out at the right moment. Things were definitely not going to be simple, but hopefully they would go smoothly enough. Maman's astral self landed beside me, I felt her metaphysical hand brush my shoulder. She was so far undetected due to the differing form of projection that The Sergeant was using. Unlike Les Magiques, he could not reach a level of projection where he could pass undetected. He may have basic concealment mastered, but his lack of magic was to his detriment. He could not work with the elements and La Mére Eternelle because of the blackness of his heart. Anyone wishing to work with the forces of good must have some good quality within. It was obvious from looking at him that he had none. I spoke to Maman telepathically, sending the message with my heart, not my head. That way no one in the room would be able to detect the message.

'Maman, when I release my left hand it will be time. At that moment rejoin your body and protect Mum and Dad. Let me fight, the clone will not know how to react without orders and The Sergeant is fading fast. Le Selleur will be my only worry and I can handle him. Don't argue, just do as I say, we will win. If this goes right, which it will, we shall have saved both mes familles.' Maman brushed my shoulder again to let me know that she had received the message and moved to her body, hovering above, waiting.

"So Lunegosse, you see, I am in the position of power. You are alone. Monique is not fit enough to help you, she has been kept prisoner for so long that she is no better off than the clone I made of her. Le Selleur is armed and waiting, and even if I do not remain here for much longer, the clone is programmed to obey his commands as well as my own. You cannot win. You may as well surrender now."

"Lana, don't listen to him. I believe in you." Dad looked at me, his eyes full of a strange conviction I had never seen in him before.

"Silence human. She cannot defeat

me. When she has surrendered I will return you and your wife home. I will release her aunt as well. If Lunegosse surrenders she will save you all. If not…" At that point The Sergeant began to flicker. His image grew fuzzy and I knew that he would not last longer than seconds. A loud snap and he was gone. I slowly released my left hand and Maman returned to her body. She did not move, just waited for me to take the first step. I turned to face Le Selleur:

"Avec tout mon coeur, j'ai attaché vous. You are bound from hurting anyone in this room. Try to do so and you will find out what will happen." He began to laugh and moved towards the clone, thinking that she was Monique. He raised his knife and it turned back on him, slicing his left arm exactly where he had intended to cut her. He tried again and the cut on his arm became deeper with the second stroke of the blade. In effect Le Selleur was of more harm to himself than anyone else in the room. I moved quickly, knowing that he may overcome the binding momentarily. His training would help him overcome it eventually and the spell would not work a second time. Maman led Mum and Dad to the centre of the room and I moved towards the clone. I may not have been able to control her, but I could still see into her mind. I projected myself into her head and delved around for the information I required. I soon discovered that the defence system and the basic controls lay within the room in which we were situated. I moved towards the console and found Le Selleur blocking me. He had released his binds and was now able to stop anyone from doing anything. He ordered the clone to attack and she moved towards Maman and my parents. He let out a gasp of shock as he realised that the real clone was not the one with my parents. I took my opportunity and dodged past him to the control panel. I reached it and began searching for the defence module.

"So you still think you can get past me?" Le Selleur grabbed my left arm and spun me round. "You are just a stupid girl. Your little binding spell couldn't hold me and I have more strength than you. Jacques Le Selleur is more than a match for a fifteen year old girl and you shall soon find out what real pain feels like." Admittedly he was strong, but I knew that I was stronger. I couldn't readily get out of the grip he had

me in and astraling would not help me as
my physical body would still be holding the
potion filled weapon. What he did not have
though, was control over my emotions. As I
watched the clone and Maman in battle, my
heart raced with fear. Fear for the lives of
the three people in the room whom I loved
and those back on the ground as well. If I
was to give in, Maman, Mum and Dad
would go home, but the torture of my
families would never stop. I had to remove
myself from Le Selleur's grip to win this part
of the fight and live to fulfil my destiny. At
that moment something inside me snapped.
I lifted Le Selleur's arm from mine with
telekinesis and raced towards the console.
Accepting my destiny had given me new
strength, and using the weapon I fired the
vial of potion into the only hole I could see
on the entire panel. I did not have time to
see if it had worked as I heard Maman
screaming for help. Le Selleur had joined the
clone in attacking them and Maman was
struggling to fend them off. I rushed to her
side, casting the binding spell on the clone as
I ran. I threw myself onto the back of the
man attacking my loved ones. I pulled his
arms away from my dad and I began kicking

him with all my might. As much as I do not
agree with physical violence I found that I
had no other choice. As I said earlier I could
no longer bind him, and with the armour he
had across his back any spell I cast would be
deflected. My kicks distracted him for long
enough to allow Maman to move away from
him. She did so and under her breath cast a
spell. He doubled in two and I was thrown
over his head. Le Selleur was crippled with
pain. Maman had cast a douleur spell and it
had hit him full force in the stomach. I
grabbed hold of Mum and Dad's hands and
dragged them over to where Maman stood.
It would take the both of us to cast the spell
to get us out of there and then that would
only work if the defence system was down.
That was the only thing I wasn't sure of, yet I
was banking that it was.

*

Le Selleur lay on the floor clutching
his stomach, the pain he must have been
feeling looked immense. He was definitely
not going to be a problem with his limited
capacity. Maman stood beside Mum, I was
beside Dad. We held our hands around

them and chanted together:

"Avec le consentment de La Mére
Eternelle,
With the consent of The Eternal Mother

Avec s'aide nous ferons prendre ces
personnes chez ils
With her aid we will take them home

La lune et le sol sont nos amis et par leur
pouvoirs nous retour
*The moon and the sun are our friends and by
their powers we return*

Au revoir de Le Sergent et vos agents
Goodbye to The Sergeant and your agents

Jusqu'à ce que la prochaine fois
Until the next time"

With that our bodies moved as one,
descending down onto the ground below the
ship, to our waiting families. The twins lit a
set of fireworks and soon the air was full
with the bangs and smoke of several dozen
rockets and we were on our way back to La
Grotte. We had experienced the first of

many battles to come.

CHAPTER ELEVEN

Au Revoir

We got safely back into La Grotte and closed the entrance off behind us. I was filled with elation and yet it all had seemed too easy. I don't know, maybe it all just felt a little anti climactic. I mean I was happy to have rescued Mum and Dad, but because I hadn't defeated The Sergeant it meant that I would have to face him again. I felt that I had failed in achieving my destiny. I knew one thing for certain though - I was absolutely shattered. For the first time in months I actually longed to be curled up in bed, and wasn't worrying about what Le Selleur and his cohorts were doing to my parents. I collapsed into one of the armchairs by the fire with the thirty-six hour clock and just enjoyed the warmth and comfort of its cushioned fabric. Mémé disappeared into the kitchen and Tim and Monique sat smiling at everyone. Catharine was happily watching the scene as Mum and Dad hugged the twins and Sam repeatedly whilst Kara gave Maman a health check. It was definitely nice to back in the safety of networked caves and even better to have all those I held dear to my heart in one place. Mémé came bustling back in with a tray full of steaming mugs of hot chocolate and another filled with all the chocolaty cakes you could imagine piled high. There were muffins, chocolate gateaux, devil's food cake and many, many more. We spent the remaining hours of the day enveloped in chocolate and hugs. At seven o'clock I made my excuses and headed down the corridor to bed. I fell onto the bed, fully clothed and fell into the first untroubled sleep I had had since arriving in La Grotte. If I dreamed that night, I couldn't tell you what I dreamt as I slept so deeply I doubt that I did.

*

I awoke the next day to find all three of my parents sitting in my bedroom.

Maman smiled as I looked at her through my sleep-blurred eyes. Dad had his arm around Mum who looked as if she had been crying. The whole scene looked very surreal. I almost thought I was still dreaming but persipacité sixiéme told me otherwise. I couldn't understand Mum's tears. I knew when she was crying with happiness, but this time her eyes were filled with sadness.

"Mum, what's wrong? You're safe now we all are. We're together again."

"Oh Lana…" She burst into tears again.

"Lana, the thing is… well, we're grateful for all you've done and we love you dearly. It's just that we know that you're going to have to leave soon." Dad looked at me and smiled weakly.

"Leave? I'm not planning on leaving. I've only just got you guys back, I'm staying for a while at least." Did they really think I was just going to up and leave after the months I had spent without them?

"Lunegosse, Lana, mon enfant. If you look deep inside you know that you…we're going to have to leave. We may have won the first battle, but you have your destiny to fulfil and we are no longer safe here. The Sergeant knows we are on the island. The entire Magique clan have to leave and we will have to do it soon." La Mére Eternelle! Of course we would have to leave. But that meant that I had to leave half of me behind, as much as I had accepted that my destiny was inevitable I could not believe it meant destroying everything I had always known. I had to tear myself away from my siblings, the parents I had known practically since birth, Catharine, Jersey. I felt my heart breaking in two. This wasn't the way I had imagined things would be before I met Mémé. I had always dreamed of the two families getting along, that I would be able to see both of them every day - childhood fantasies.

*

The next few days were the hardest of my life. The days when I was planning to rescue Mum and Dad had been easy by comparison. I had begun to pack my belongings, my room was scattered with cardboard boxes half full with books and ornaments, suitcases containing half my clothes, I had begun to see the room for what

it was, a cave. Mum sat in the guest
bedroom she was sharing with Dad, crying
all day long. I had barely seen her. Dad was
helping everyone with the packing, he had
always insisted on keeping busy rather than
deal with the emotions he was feeling. As I
placed the photos of my adoptive family in
one of the boxes the tears streamed down my
cheeks. This wasn't the way it was meant to
be. Catharine had been helping me pack on
her weekend visits, but it was becoming
harder to see her knowing that soon I would
be leaving her behind for an undeterminable
amount of time. We became best friends at
primary school and have never fallen out or
been separated for longer than a few months,
now we were facing possibly years apart. I
knew that our friendship would survive, but
I was so used to her having my back and me
having hers that leaving her behind was
almost worse than leaving Mum, Dad, Sam
and the twins. I looked around the room as I
packed. There were so many friendship
trinkets Catharine had given me still
unpacked. I couldn't bear to leave them
behind. Stupid things like a Care Bear
figurine she had given me in reception after I
had fallen in the playground and fractured

my left thighbone were sitting on the shelves. I took them down with a form of reverence and carefully wrapped them in tissue before packing them in one large box. I taped the box and labelled it with our childhood nicknames for each other - 'La and Catty'. It may seem silly to you that a fifteen year old would label a box like that, but in my heart that's how I felt. Outwardly I may have been fifteen and a half, but inwardly I was no longer a teenager, I had faced too much to claim that I was just a child anymore.

*

Dinner that night was hard to cope with. Everyone sat down in silence; no one could bring themselves to talk about the impending journey. I thought that Mémé would have taken back the matriarchal powers by now but she hadn't so whilst everyone else sat not looking at each other, heads pointed towards their meals, I could hear every single thought running through their heads; including those of my adoptive family and that increased the weight on my heart further. Mum's thoughts weren't that different from usual. She sobbed in thought as well as outwardly, words occasionally becoming clear, things like 'my baby' and 'going away'. Dad's thoughts were more coherent 'My darling little girl, all grown up, off to fulfil her destiny. I'll miss you Princess.' Well he may not have been able to outwardly express his feelings, but Dad definitely was rather soppy inwardly. Maman was thinking words in French that I dare not write down. Let's just say that she wasn't at all happy about me being torn in two. Tim and Kara were having a telepathic conversation about the move. Kara seemed fairly happy. Apparently she had split with her boyfriend, something I would have known about had I not been so focused on other things. He hadn't been too happy with the idea of her not being able to spend as much time with him as he wanted her to. The twins were both forlorn over the whole situation. This time neither of them was joking it off. John had tears in his eyes, including his mind's eye. I had always been the perfect little sis in his eyes - I liked playing the tomboy and he suddenly realised I had grown out of that phase. James wasn't actually thinking much, he repeatedly had the words 'She can't go' running through his head. Monique was obviously not looking forward to the prospect of travelling the galaxies after her last experience in space. I didn't need to read her thoughts to tell that one. Sam was crying inwardly as well as Mum. It was only in recent years that she and I had begun to understand each other and become friends rather than sisters. Mémé's thoughts were the most confusing it was all rather jumbled and the only words I heard properly were '…must tell her…can't do it now…' The 'her' she was referring to had to be me because whenever she looked at me her eyes broke contact very quickly. What she was thinking about was obviously troubling her. All in all when we left each other's company and headed to our separate bedrooms, everyone made their way with a heavy laden heart.

*

I awoke with a start about two and a half hours after I had finally fallen asleep. Something was definitely amiss. There were eleven of us within La Grotte, including me but I wasn't the only one awake. Mémé's life force had moved back into the primary living room. I got out of bed, put a dressing gown on and headed down the corridor until I reached the room where Mémé was pacing the length of the largest rug. She did not notice me until she turned back towards the hall and she jumped as I came into her sight.

"Lunegosse, what... you should be asleep." If anyone should have been asleep it was her, the bags under her eyes could have been used to pack the entire contents of La Grotte and then some.

"Sleep? That's a laugh! How can I when all I can hear inside my head is the jumbled thoughts of everyone else and if I do drift off I get woken with a start because someone isn't where they ought to be? I'll be glad when you take these powers away from me! I am grateful for the loan but please can you take them back now, I'm kinda sick of having them!" Maybe now wasn't the time for honesty but I was too tired to pussyfoot around.

"I've been meaning to talk to you about that. You see the thing is, I cannot take them back and you cannot give them to me. When the powers are handed over they can only be handed to the one who is meant to have them. What I am trying to say is that you will now have the powers until it is time for your oldest daughter to have them. They are yours and by there is nothing you or I or anyone else for that matter can do about it. I am sorry my child but there we have it. La Mére Eternelle has deemed it is you who must now protect the family and rule our homeland when you have fulfilled the prophecy. It is another weight that you must bear, and one I will endeavour to help you do." Most teenagers at that point would probably have started shouting for joy at the top of their lungs or looked confused at the fact an adult was handing them the reins. Me on the other hand, instead of getting angry, instead of yelling at Mémé because she had saddled me with more than I wanted...I just sat down head in hands and laughed. Laughed because there was nothing else I could do. If I wasn't laughing I would have been crying. There was no point in getting angry because that wouldn't solve anything, no point in crying because I would have become an emotional wreck. Staying silent didn't seem appropriate and there were no words to describe how I was feeling. Laughter seemed to be my only option.

"Ma chéri I'm sorry I had to tell you this, and I'm sorry you thought that I had handed you the powers of my own free will and could take them back. I should have told you when they transferred to you but I felt that you had enough on your plate as it was. If I could have I would have held off, allowed you more of a chance to explore your other powers. I would have liked to allow you to wait. I thought Kara was next in line for them as she is my eldest daughter, but that is not the way things were planned. You are the most powerful Magique for eons and that, I believe, is why you now are the Matriarch of this family. One day you will be able to reach your full potential and understand your abilities fully. Until that day I will do as is fit for the departing Matriarch and guide you. Oh my darling!" She sat next to me and wrapped her arms around me. So neither of us had a choice in the matter, this was how our lives were to play out. Whilst my ancestor had predicted that I would have the power to end the tyranny of The Sergeant's dictatorship, she had not predicted this. But looking at it now, I can see that the two go hand in hand.

After all, who ever heard of a saviour who in one way or another did not become a great ruler? The question racing through my mind was would I become a great ruler or would I fail?

*

Neither of us went back to bed that night. Together we continued to pack the items in the first living room and kitchen. Talking all the while of past events and how soon we would have to leave and I would have to face the toughest challenges that my destiny threw at me. It was definitely not a night full of laughter, not even the hysterical sort that I had originally broken into. When the others came through for breakfast, all that was left in the living room was furniture and the thirty-six hour clock. There was enough food and utensils in the kitchen for the rest of the day, but otherwise everything was packed. The only major packing left to be done was the library and the rest of our personal effects. Soon we would have to leave and that was the hardest thing imaginable, not least because I would miss those left behind. But it was also because I

had come to look on La Grotte as home now
and leaving the place that I felt so secure in
was a wrench. It was and still is the one
place where both my families became united
and where we all shared memories. As we
ate breakfast I tried to keep the conversation
away from the subject. Instead I talked
about stupid things. I got Mum and Dad
telling tales of me growing up and Mémé
talking about when Maman and the others
were little. We all laughed when we heard
how Kara had had an imaginary friend
called Sasa that she had invited to every
meal and had insisted that Mémé make up
one of the camp beds in her room for her.
Kara blushed a rather vivid shade of scarlet
at that point. Mum told the tale of how I had
fallen asleep under the glass-topped coffee
table one Christmas Eve and woken up at
five in the morning and started opening all
my presents. My turn to turn a rather
different colour from usual! It was a good
breakfast all in all. Moods had lightened and
I had succeeded in adding a bit of fun into
what otherwise would have been another
meal where everyone sat in silence too afraid
to say anything. As Dad and Tim took the
things through and began washing up,

Catharine turned up. Was it Saturday already? Time had flown past. We headed into my room and she helped me finish packing. We were both aware that today was the day we would say goodbye, but neither of us was willing to say it. Instead we talked about other things, like what was going on in the outside world.

"You'll never guess who's been expelled for having an affair with Mr Le Sueur!"

"Who's Mr Le Sueur?"

"You know, that new teacher that joined in September, the one we all thought would get together with Miss Carols!"

"Oh him! Well who got expelled then?"

"Cassie Monroe!"

"No way! I mean she was the most popular girl in school, and he's like thirty-five at least! Oh that is so disgusting! And yet oddly satisfying! I bet her dad through an epically proportioned fit! He's one of the best-respected men in the island and his daughter has turned out to be a proper little tramp! I mean we all knew it of course and now the whole of Jersey does. This is too much!"

"Wanna know the best bit?"

"Go on."

"They ran off together. Well she's now sixteen (you know she got put back a year) they eloped to Gretna Green. Her mother's been destroyed by it all. And to make matters worse her dad's stopped her mum from seeing her."

"That's horrible. I mean I know Cassie's a prat but her poor mother! I was separated from Maman long enough to know that that just isn't fair. What's happened to him? I mean he got sacked right?"

"Actually he resigned before they eloped. Neither have been seen or heard from since." I felt for what I was sure would be the last time, normal. There's that word again! Funny how it occasionally creeps up on you isn't it. It was in that moment that I realised that normal is a word that covers a lot of things. Before meeting Mémé it was normal for me to be bullied at school and have very few friends. After moving to La Grotte it became normal for me to practice magic. And soon it would be normal for me to be Matriarch. Funny isn't it? I mean how different things are normal to different people.

The morning passed swiftly and soon we were all eating salad in the study among piles of boxes and books. Mum couldn't believe how much of it the twins were eating. And Dad just looked from them to me and broke into the first true smile I had seen on his face in ages. This was the last room to pack apart from the kitchen bits that we would need for dinner and we were almost done. The reality was hitting me fast and that was more intimidating than knowing that the fate of more than just my family rested in my hands and always would.

*

Looking around at the boxes that had all been assembled in the primary living room after dinner, I noticed that we hadn't packed the clock. I walked over to the mantelpiece on which it stood and lifted it from its position. Underneath it, in the wood, was engraved something in French. It looked as if it had been there since the place had been completed and made me wonder if

the clock had been too. The inscription read
"*Si tu trouverai c'ette inscription, petite-fille de
Lahela, savoir que tes ancêtres sont avec tu
toujours. Tu n'est pas seule.* (If you find this
inscription, granddaughter of Lahela, know
that your ancestors are always with you.
You are never alone.) It gave me comfort
knowing that they had thought of me when
making La Grotte habitable. Admittedly it
was kinda freaky to know that they had left
a hidden message for me within the walls of
the family secret home before I was born, but
all the same it was nice. I put the clock in the
top of one of the boxes and sat waiting for
the others to join me in the lounge. All that
remained was furniture and that in itself
made the room. At the moment, however, it
added to the oddness because it was all
pushed against one wall and covered with
dustsheets. Maybe my family would never
return to this place. I could see it remaining
empty for years to come, possibly millennia.
It was a peculiar feeling knowing that in a
few moments I would be leaving for what
could be the last time within my life span.
And as much as I wanted to cry I couldn't. I
did not want the others to see me that way. I
needed to be strong for them and strong for

myself, otherwise I would not be able to move on to the next inevitable step in my life. It was time for me to take control of my emotions. Not as The Sergeant had managed to do with Le Selleur, but to know when was the right time to release them.

*

When we had all searched every last nook and cranny for forgotten items, we assembled at the foot of the stairs. I moved half the boxes up the stairs using telekinesis and the other Magiques did the same but with their wands and a rather handy moving spell. Dad's work van was parked at the entrance and it was soon packed to the hilt with our belongings. Mémé had given him directions to where we were heading and he sped off. The rest of us surveyed the landscape one last time before shutting the entrance and saying our final goodbyes to what had become home. Each Magique held hands and formed a circle around Mum and the others. Within seconds we were travelling towards Bel Royal Beach in a whirl of colour and wind using a variation of the spell Maman and I had used to transport

Mum and Dad off of The Sergeant's ship. In no time at all we were standing at the edge of the sea. The waves lapped at our feet. It was high tide and from where we stood against the wall we were invisible in the encroaching darkness. Dad pulled up in the van and wolf-whistled to let us know he had arrived. He opened the back doors and came down to join us. Hugs and kisses goodbye began to fly as Mémé looked at the sea and a mass began to rise up. It was black and yet white at the same time. Made of a metal I had never seen before. Written on the side in a blue that was deeper than any you could imagine was written the word: *Victoire.* The name felt right, it somehow seemed beautiful to me. The holding door at the bottom opened as the ship hovered just above the water and we emptied the van and put the boxes in the hold. Then was the time for final goodbyes. Mum burst into sobs as she hugged me one last time. Catharine smiled and slipped something into my pocket. I went to reach for it but she shook her head, she wanted me to open it once on board. I didn't need telepathy to tell me that one. I hugged my siblings and Dad and then turned to face the ship. Time to go. One more look back and a group hug and I joined my biological family who had already boarded. The ship rose into the air and I stood on the bridge and saw my last glimpse of Jersey. I reached into my pocket and took out what Catharine had placed in it. I discovered to some amusement and sadness that she had given me another charm for the friendship bracelet she had bought me in year seven. A star with a small image of Jersey in it. She must have had it specially made. The tears welled in my eyes as I said my last silent goodbye.

EPILOGUE

Well there we have it, the beginning of a story that I am not ready to complete yet. Yes I have more to tell you and indeed will have more to tell you. But I do not want to overload your mind. You are my heir, you are getting ready to become the Matriarch of a most amazing family and if everything has gone right the ruler of a free world. That may sound like a daunting prospect, still is for me as I write this, but I know one thing for sure. I will be with you always, I do not know fully in what capacity, but if our ancestors believed it then so do I. Remember always that you are loved by those you call family and by me. For whilst I may never have met you, you are my blood and that creates an unbreakable bond between us.

I will finish here for now. I'll write again soon and let you know how things progress, after all I promised an account of how you came to be where you are now, and that I shall, as soon as I know more myself. So for now take care ma Cheri.

Toujours mon amour,
A bientôt,

Lunegosse Mathilde Cornique Le Monnier (Lana)

###

About the Author

N. A. Le Brun was born and raised in Jersey, Channel Islands, off the coast of France, so it seems natural that the first of the Lunegosse books is set primarily on the island. This book has been re-written many times since its first draft in 2000, and is finally ready for an audience.

Printed in Great Britain
by Amazon